D1515772

GWENDOLEN

Also by Clare Darcy

GWENDOLEN

BY

CLARE DARCY

WALKER AND COMPANY
NEW YORK

First published in the United States of America in 1978 by the Walker Publishing Company, Inc.

Published simultaneously in Canada by Beaverbooks, Limited, Pickering, Ontario.

ISBN: 0-8027-0605-3

Library of Congress Catalog Card Number: 78-58345

Printed in the United States of America

10 9 8 7 6 5 4 3 2 1

One

The scene in the breakfast parlour at Brightleaves on an agreeably warm morning in late June of the year 1814 was not one that would have occasioned comment in any gentleman's house in Gloucestershire. To be sure, the Turkey carpet and the red camlet curtains at the large window overlooking a fine orchard of White Damsons and May Dukes were distinctly shabby; the family portraits over the sideboard were dim with neglect; and the table linens were so fragile from long use that they had had to be mended in a number of places. But the three ladies seated about the small mahogany table had an undeniable look of deserving better things, and would not have appeared out of place (in spite of their rather *démodé* apparel) in the breakfast parlour even of so exalted a house as the Duke of Tardiff's magnificent neighbouring mansion at Beauworth.

Lady Otilia Quarters, the mistress of Brightleaves, attired in a somewhat exotic Parisian dressing gown that had descended to her from her sister, Lady Priscilla Drumm, was presiding over the coffee urn. She turned over, with an air of businesslike disinterest, the small heap of letters comprising the morning post, most of which, she knew from long experience, would consist of urgent requests for the payment of various domestic bills. Opposite her sat two of her three daughters, Gwendolen, the eldest, a rather tall girl, fair, but with flyaway black brows that gave her heart-shaped face a good deal of character, and Campaspe, the youngest, just emerging, at seventeen, from what her mama considered a regrettably hoydenish girlhood.

Lady Otilia's second daughter, Jane, was at the moment en route from London, where she had been enjoying the advantages of the Season under the aegis of Lady Priscilla; and Lady Otilia's husband, Mr. Hugh Quarters, had long since consumed his own hearty breakfast and left the house. Being in the habit of rising at five during the hunting season, he was unused to breakfasting with his family, in whom he was, on the whole, rather less interested than he was in his horses and his hounds, considering that they had all signally failed him; his wife by producing only offspring of the female sex and his daughters by committing the crime of being girls.

At the moment, Gwendolen and Campaspe were engaged in speculation as to what tales of London splendours they might expect to hear from Jane when she arrived at Brightleaves later that day, for her letters had been tantalisingly brief, the excuse being constantly pleaded that the ceaseless round of evening-parties, routs, receptions, and breakfasts to which Lady Priscilla's position in the *ton* had procured her invitations allowed her no time for correspondence. Her sisters, left with nothing more exciting than the tame and familiar rural pastimes of Brightleaves, had endeavoured to be understanding, but there was no denying that they were exceedingly eager to hear Jane's account of this most glorious of London Seasons, the Season of the Great Peace Celebration, when the metropolis swarmed with foreign royalties, and one might expect to see the Tsar of Russia, the King of Prussia, or at least the Grand Duchess of Oldenburg whenever one entered a *ton* saloon or attended a subscription ball at Almack's.

In all of this the two young ladies at Brightleaves had up to the moment shared only in the form of their perusal of the dispatches in the *Morning Post* and of Jane's all-too-succinct letters, which had run more or less in the style of: *"Aunt and I attended Lady Castlereagh's ball last evening. Tsar Alexander was present, with his sister, the Grand Duchess. He is excessively handsome."*

"Excessively handsome, indeed!" Campaspe had grumbled, upon receipt of this unsatisfactory missive. "As if everyone in England didn't know that already! If only Jane weren't so depressingly *good*! I am sure it never enters her head to repeat even the mildest gossip, and as for scandal—! But she might at least have told us what the Grand Duchess was wearing."

Gwendolen had said judicially that, for her part, she considered the very large new bonnets the Grand Duchess had brought into fashion exceedingly ugly, but she confessed that she, too, felt a good deal of disappointment over Jane's deficiencies as a correspondent. As she had been used from childhood, however, to constituting herself her gentle younger sister's champion, she permitted no further aspersions to be cast upon her by Campaspe, informing her instead that, since she intended to be a soldier's wife, she had best forget the frivolities of the fashionable world and concentrate her attention upon mastering at least the rudiments of domestic economy.

This was in reference to Campaspe's engagement—not very favourably regarded by Lady Otilia—to a young lieutenant in the Light division, Neil Fairhall, the second son of a neighbouring landowner. Admittedly, Campaspe was not the "Beauty" of the family—a distinction that undeniably belonged to Jane—but she had recently blossomed out of her puppy fat into a most engagingly attractive young lady, with a small, robust, supple figure, a dazzling complexion, and sparkling blue eyes, and Lady Otilia, dreaming of London for her as she had for Jane, had anticipated that she might at least bring a baronet into the family.

She could, however, have no real objection to the proposed match beyond the extreme youth of the two young people, and as they had promised to be sensible and not even to think of marriage until Neil had obtained his promotion—and also as she knew Campaspe's exceedingly obstinate, not to say headstrong, nature— she had, like the other parents involved, reluctantly given her consent.

She had had no such scruples in bestowing her blessing, approximately a year before, upon Gwendolen's betrothal to Captain Henry Belville, R.N., for Gwendolen had been all of twenty at the time and Captain Belville a man of one-and-thirty, with a highly successful naval career that had added a good deal of prize money to the already considerable fortune he had inherited.

It was true that Gwendolen's acquaintance with him

4

had been very brief, covering no more than a fortnight he had spent on leave two years before in the neighbourhood with his distant relations, the Rutledges, and that their courtship had been conducted entirely by correspondence between Brightleaves and the various Mediterranean stations where Captain Belville had been posted during the war. But Gwendolen, like Campaspe, had a mind of her own, as well as the sort of practical nature that Lady Otilia, herself a hopelessly muddleheaded romantic, had never felt herself capable of interfering with, and Lady Otilia had every confidence that when Captain Belville finally appeared once more in Gloucestershire there would be a discreetly fashionable wedding, followed by a highly satisfactory married life, in store for her eldest daughter.

"Gwendolen," she had once confided to her friend Mrs. Rutledge, "always succeeds in managing *everything* to perfection"—with which statement Mrs. Rutledge, who had seen Gwendolen succeed in getting herself engaged to the highly eligible Captain Belville under the very nose of her own daughter, Evelina, was only too ready to agree.

In speaking thus of Gwendolen's engagement, however, Mrs. Rutledge and Lady Otilia were doing her a considerable injustice. The truth was that Gwendolen had managed nothing in regard to Captain Belville, but instead had fallen head over ears in love with him, merely substituting his tall, high-shouldered figure for the rather less impressive one of Lord Nelson, whom she had heroworshipped since she had been a schoolgirl, and charitably overlooking the fact that he had all his arms and eyes.

Few people, in fact, suspected that the self-possessed,

attractive eldest of the Quarters girls, with her fair good looks and her frank manners, was as much a romantic at heart as her mama; but she was not Lady Otilia's daughter for nothing, and, far from considering her engagement to Captain Belville in a practical light as an excellent match, thought of herself rather as a more decorous Lady Hamilton, giving all for love to her naval hero, though, as there was no prior Mrs. Belville in the picture, the comparison was perhaps inapt.

At any rate, she was soon to have the reward of having waited through two interminable years of war for her lover's return. Captain Belville's ship was shortly expected to reach Portsmouth, whence it was to be anticipated that he would proceed with all due speed and regard for naval orders to the arms of his betrothed. The fact that young Lieutenant Fairhall had also recently arrived in England after a period of recuperation from a rather serious wound he had received in the battle of Toulouse, and was now completing his recovery in Gloucestershire on his father's estate, meant, therefore, that Lady Otilia would soon have the felicity of displaying *two* engaged daughters and their betrotheds to the neighbourhood—a prospect that she could not but regard with some complacency.

"Now if only Jane were to contract an eligible alliance—" she was fond of saying to her husband, who never paid the least heed to her, being far more interested in the mating of his horses than in that of his daughters. "*Not*," she would add proudly, "that one need feel the least doubt of that, for Pris writes that she is having the greatest success in London, and that it will not surprise her to see her made a marchioness before the year is out."

6

Prophetic words, it appeared; or at least Lady Priscilla's hints might have prepared Lady Otilia for what she was to read that morning in one of the letters that lay beside her plate—though if they *had* prepared her, the gasp she uttered upon perusing its initial lines gave no hint of it. Gwendolen and Campaspe looked up from their own breakfasts to see their mama staring at the sheet of elegant cream-laid notepaper with an expression upon her face that might have betokened a seizure of some sort, utter horror, or rapturous delight. With Lady Otilia, it was difficult to tell; being Welsh, and with a strong Celtic flair for the dramatic, she always overplayed her emotions.

"What is it, Mama?" Gwendolen enquired, prepared for anything, but unwilling to commit herself to concern until she knew the reason for her volatile parent's perturbation.

Lady Otilia raised her eyes, which had been fixed upon the letter before her as if she had been mesmerised by the words she had read there, and Gwendolen saw a beatific smile slowly appear upon her still rather pretty, plump face.

"My dears!" she ejaculated. "You will never guess! Dear, dear Jane! A marchioness! Oh, I shall never forgive myself for having given in to your papa's wishes and allowed her to be christened *Jane*, only because of that odious great-aunt of his who was going to die and leave us a very pretty fortune, only she never did, and lived on for *ages*, and then it was no more than three hundred pounds we had of her, and your papa spent every penny of it on a mare named Sparkler—"

"*Mama!*" It was Campaspe who interrupted, with an appearance of the greatest impatience and—oddly, it

7

would have seemed—even of consternation upon her face. "*Do* give over rambling on forever about great-aunts and Papa's horses and tell us what is in the letter. Is it from Aunt Pris? Is—is Jane engaged to a *marquis*?"

"Not to say actually *engaged*, my dear," said Lady Otilia, collecting herself with some difficulty, it appeared, and rearranging the lace frill on her dressing gown, which, as Lady Priscilla was somewhat taller than she, had a distracting way of slipping off her shoulders in a rather *dégagé* manner. "But as near it as makes no difference! Lyndale, if you will believe it!" She enunciated the name reverentially. "Estates in Derbyshire and in Kent, Pris says, and at least fifty thousand a year! *And* a marquis, of course, my loves! He is to come to Gloucestershire at once and request your papa's permission to pay his addresses to her! Pris says it is all quite, quite settled; she has had a long conversation with him—"

"He is coming *here*?"

This time it was Gwendolen's turn to look dismayed as her eyes took in at a glance the shabby red curtains, the faded carpet, and the Lowestoft ware upon the table, which, though it had been very pretty once, now displayed for all to see the chips and cracks of its long service. The notion of entertaining in such surroundings a member of the highest ranks of the nobility, who was possessed, in addition, of so large a fortune that he must expect to have everything about him in the first style of elegance, might not strike housewifely terror into Lady Otilia's breast, for she was well known to dwell in a vague, romantic world of her own, in which such details as cracked plates and mended table linens were generously overlooked.

But Gwendolen's more practical nature saw things

8

with a clearer eye. It would be appallingly difficult, she was well aware, with their meagre staff and limited means, to entertain properly a gentleman of the Marquis's high position, and she was therefore greatly relieved to hear her mama say, as she once more consulted Lady Priscilla's letter, "No, no, *not* here at Brightleaves, my dear; he is to stay at Beauworth, your aunt writes. He is cousin to the Duke, you know." She added triumphantly, "I daresay it will be quite impossible for the Duke to ignore us any longer, now that dear Jane is to be betrothed to Lyndale" —for it had long been a sore point with her that, owing to a quarrel that had occurred years before between Mr. Hugh Quarters and the Duke, she and her daughters were never invited to Beauworth.

The quarrel had come about as a result of the fact that the Duke, who knew everything about his neighbours' business owing to having a very large and efficient staff who would have been sacked without mercy if they had failed him even in the smallest detail, had discovered that Mr. Quarters's affairs had got at that time into such a tangled state that the only way out for him appeared to be to sell Brightleaves and its remaining land. It was land that the Duke had long coveted, embracing as it did the finest trout-stream in that part of the county, and he had accordingly lost no time in making an offer for it.

The offer, however, had unfortunately been received by Mr. Quarters—notoriously a gentleman of a quick and unpredictable temper—in much the same spirit in which a devout Christian might receive an offer from the devil for the purchase of his soul. Brushing aside the Duke's man of business, who had come to Brightleaves as his noble master's emissary, he had ridden over to

Beauworth on one of the splendid coverhacks with which, in spite of the Duke's unlimited means, he always managed to take the shine off the inmates of his ducal neighbour's stables, and had demanded audience with the Duke himself. High words had then passed between them — including, as had later been relayed by a sharp-eared footman to a breathlessly attentive audience in the Hall, a threat by Mr. Quarters to pitch the Duke's man of business into the millpond if he ever came to Brightleaves upon such an errand again, and an equally disagreeable promise by the Duke to "ruin" Mr. Quarters.

Fortunately, neither of these interesting events had come to pass. Mr. Quarters, by certain mysterious dealings with Messrs. Smith and Brown, the well-known London moneylenders, had contrived not to be obliged to sell Brightleaves to the Duke or to anyone else; the Duke had made no more offers for it; and a state of armed neutrality had now existed for several years between the opposing parties, in which Brightleaves and Beauworth mutually ignored each other socially.

What the Duke of Tardiff might or might not do now as a result of his cousin's becoming engaged to Miss Jane Quarters was not, however, a matter that appeared to interest that young lady's sisters at the moment. Indeed, the news of the projected betrothal, far from arousing the same pleasurable excitement in their breasts that it had in their mama's, appeared rather to have thrown them into a distinctly grave and, in Campaspe's case, even a much perturbed mood.

"But, Mama, Jane *can't* —" she burst out impetuously, as Lady Otilia ceased speaking; but Gwendolen checked her with a warning glance.

"What has Jane to say to all this?" she herself went on

to enquire in a more temperate tone of Lady Otilia. "Is there no word from her in Aunt Pris's letter?"

"Oh, my dear, she will be thrown into transports, of course!" Lady Otilia said largely. "Naturally, she has not written herself, since Lyndale spoke to your aunt only after Jane had set out on her journey—and, indeed, it would scarcely be becoming in her to discuss the matter before Lord Lyndale has received her papa's permission to pay his addresses to her! Jane has always been the soul of propriety, you know," she concluded proudly.

Campaspe again opened her mouth to speak, but was once more forestalled by Gwendolen.

"Yes, she has," she agreed to Lady Otilia's last statement. "Which makes it seem more than a little odd—doesn't it?—that she should have attracted the interest of a man like Lyndale. You must remember, Mama, what a great deal of tittle-tattle there was when he succeeded to the title a year or so ago; it made a stir even in such a quiet, out-of-the-way place as this. A man who has spent the past dozen years in—is it Morocco? —Algeria?—at any rate, quite out of the way of civilisation, and whose adventures there would seem to make some of Lord Byron's heroes appear pale by comparison—surely it appears very odd for him to fix his choice on a quiet, inexperienced girl like Jane—"

"Not at all! Not in the least, my dear!" said Lady Otilia roundly. "Indeed, it frequently happens, I believe, that a gentleman who has led a life of—shall we say, varied experiences?—acquires the wisdom in the course of those experiences to realise that a carefully reared girl like Jane will make him the most satisfactory sort of wife. And then she is so very beautiful, you know! I am sure we need feel no surprise at any conquest she has made!" She rose, gathering up the sheets of her letter. "But I must not stay talking here forever," she said briskly, "for I promised Mrs. Rutledge I should call this morning, and it might very well be that I may stop in for a moment at the Rectory as well. I daresay you will wish to come with me, my dears? It is a lovely day; I am sure we shall all enjoy the walk."

She drifted out of the room on a flutter of her exotic draperies, while Campaspe sat gazing at her elder sister in despair.

"She will tell *everyone!*" she exclaimed tragically. "Gwen, what *are* we to do? Jane *can't* marry this—this *Bluebeard!*"

Gwendolen smiled. "Oh no, Cammie—that is coming it much too strong!" she said. "There is no reason in the world for you to call Lord Lyndale a Bluebeard. As far as I have ever heard, he hasn't had so much as one other wife, far less murdered her, even though one *does* hear it rumoured that he engaged in every activity from brigandage to lion-hunting with sultans and sheikhs while he was in that outlandish part of the world. And of course Jane can marry him if she wishes to—"

"But she *doesn't* wish to!" Campaspe interrupted mutinously. "She is in love with Alain; you know that quite as well as I do!"

"I know she *fancied* she was in love with him when she left here to go to London," Gwendolen corrected her. "Alain de Combray is a very agreeable and attractive young man, but, after all, one meets a great many attractive and agreeable young men in London during the Season, and perhaps Alain does not seem quite such a paragon to Jane now. And you know he hasn't a penny to bless himself with, apart from the wages he receives as the Duke's secretary."

"Jane is *not* mercenary!" said Campaspe hotly. "*That* would not weight with her in the least—not when she has given her heart!"

Gwendolen could have wished that her young sister was not such an avid reader of lending-library novels, for she felt that, whether Jane had forgotten young M. de Combray or not in the giddy whirl of her first London Season, she, Gwendolen, was going to have a difficult time of it to prevent her romantically inclined youngest sister from building the affair up into a high tragedy, with embarrassing results for everyone concerned. She herself was rather inclined to believe that Jane, swayed by the pressing attentions of an older, more experienced lover and influenced by what must certainly have been Lady Priscilla's decided approval of the match, had allowed herself to be persuaded into acceptance of it; for she knew her sister's docile, conformable temper.

On the other hand, however, Jane had from childhood been constant in her affections, and Gwendolen could not forget her sister's first blushing confession, made almost six months ago now, of her partiality for young M. de Combray, whom she had met at the Assemblies at Cheltenham during the winter. There had been no question of an engagement, for Alain de Combray, whose family had lost everything in France during the Revolution, was not in a position to think of taking a wife—added to which, the mere fact of his being French, to say nothing of his being in the Duke's employ, would have been sufficient to make him *persona non grata* to Mr. Quarters.

13

Jane had therefore not even confided her preference for young M. de Combray to her mother, had behaved towards him with exemplary propriety whenever she had met him in public (although this had not prevented one or two brief, tear-stained private meetings of a more passionate nature), and had meekly allowed herself to be swept off, as the Beauty of the family and the only unengaged daughter, to London for the Season by Lady Priscilla.

One might, Gwendolen thought in slight vexation, know better how matters stood if Jane had been more communicative in her letters; but, as she had never mentioned either Lord Lyndale or Alain de Combray in any of them, one was left very much in the dark.

Two

Gwendolen succeeded, however, in curbing Campaspe's ill-advised desire to inform Lady Otilia of the attachment that had existed between Jane and M. de Combray by dint of persuading her that they ought to do nothing until they had had the opportunity to discuss the matter with Jane herself later that day. Then, feeling the need to be alone for a time to think over the whole perplexing matter, she cried off both from accompanying her mother to call on the Rutledges and from accepting Campaspe's not very pressing invitation to accompany *her* on a visit to young Lieutenant Fairhall at the Manor, just beyond the village. She was well aware, at any rate, that Neil Fairhall would far rather have Campaspe to himself for half an hour than be obliged to engage in polite conversation with her elder sister; and Lady Otilia, too, would be happier spreading her hints of

15

future glories for the house of Quarters without the constraint that would be occasioned by her daughter's obvious lack of sympathy with such premature disclosures.

She did not intend, however, to remain indoors with her troublesome thoughts on such a fine day, and when she had seen her mother and sister go off, and had called in the cook to discuss the menu for dinner — a task that Lady Otilia habitually delegated to her — she donned her oldest bonnet and a pair of stout shoes and left the house herself for a morning ramble through the lanes.

For a time, thoughts of Jane occupied her mind, but, as was not unusual on those rare occasions when she found herself alone and at leisure, her mind soon reverted to Captain Henry Belville, R.N. Like Jane, the Captain left much to be desired as a correspondent, favouring a succinct style that might have done very well for his logbook but had its drawbacks as descriptive prose. But Gwendolen was accustomed to filling in the gaps in his accounts of his life at sea with her own imagination, and saw cannons belching smoke and flame, boarding-parties meeting with the clash and ring of glinting steel, and sails and rigging collapsing under a hail of shot, when perusing even the driest of his missives.

She had lost herself now, as she strolled slowly along a narrow lane hedged with straight-set quick embroidered with wild rose and blackberry, in an agreeable dream of her coming reunion with her naval hero when a rapid beat of hooves behind her startled her abruptly out of her reverie. She glanced quickly over her shoulder and at the same moment saw, rounding a bend in the lane behind her with never a check in its breakneck pace, a smart curricle drawn by a magnificent team of chestnuts thundering down upon her. There was no time, she realised instantly, for the driver to rein in his horses before they would be upon her, and, with that realisation, her sense of self-preservation immediately took control. The lane was narrow, and ditched on either side, but self-preservation was regardless of such difficulties, and she found herself the next instant sliding in a most un-dignified manner down the grassy side of the ditch, to end up at the bottom, her bonnet askew, her dimity frock grass-stained and muddy, and her temper entirely out of control.

She had got to her feet and was attempting to scramble up the rather steep side of the ditch when she became aware that the curricle had been halted and that the driver, a tall, dark-haired man in a smart box-coat of white drab, had thrown the reins to his groom and, jumping down from his seat, was now striding rapidly towards her. Their eyes met, hers flashing with in-dignation, his full of a kind of hard concern—but the next moment, to her astonished fury, the concern had quite vanished and an expression of definite amusement had sprung up instead in the very blue eyes that were sur-veying her.

She ceased her efforts to climb the bank and gave him a scorching glance.

"Yes, I daresay, it *is* very amusing—to *you!*" she said scathingly. "Is it your custom to run people down on the public roads, sir, for the pleasure of enjoying their discomfiture? You will permit me to say that I don't ad-mire your taste in jests!"

"No, I expect you don't—but it wasn't done with malice aforethought, you know!" the stranger said, but not in the least with the air of apologising for his actions, so that her wrath remained quite unmollified. "How the devil was I to know there would be anyone wandering along this lane? It must be half a dozen miles since I've met so much as a cow! Here—give me your hand," he commanded, reaching his own down to her.

She took it reluctantly, and was drawn securely up the bank to the lane.

"And someone, moreover," he continued on with what he had been saying before this interruption had occurred, "with her head so much in the clouds that she wouldn't hear a carriage approaching until it was upon her!" The blue eyes, again full of frank amusement, were surveying her with a mercilessly candid glance such as she never remembered to have received from any gentleman before. "You'd best straighten your bonnet," he advised her, with a directness that matched the glance, as she opened her mouth to speak. "I can see you're preparing to rake me down, and I doubt I shall be able to attend to you with proper gravity if I'm obliged to stand here looking at you while you present such a very peculiar spectacle!"

With the wind quite taken out of her sails, and suddenly acutely conscious of her stained, crumpled frock and generally dishevelled appearance, Gwendolen seized the offending bonnet with both hands and set it firmly upon her head.

"Sir—!" She gritted out from between set teeth. "Sir—! You are—"

"Insufferable?" the stranger obligingly prompted her, as she struggled for words. "Impudent? Offensive?"

"All three!" she flashed. "If you were a gentleman—"

"Well, I am, you know," the stranger remarked conversationally, "though I daresay I'm a bit out of practice just now. You see, I have returned to England only very

18

recently, after upwards of a dozen years spent abroad, and one rather forgets all the little niceties—"

"A—a dozen years!" Gwendolen repeated. A horrid suspicion suddenly entered her mind; she stood staring up into that bronzed face—surely too deeply tanned to be the result of any northern sun—and thought in despair, "Good God, it can't be! But I daresay it is! Jane's marquis! Oh, *dear*!"

All the same, she was still really in too much of a flame to care whether this uncivil stranger was Lyndale or not. He *was* insufferable, and impudent, and offensive, she told herself, and if Jane preferred him to Alain de Combray, she had certainly more hair than wit.

The Marquis—if it was the Marquis—was looking down at her now with a rather quizzically expectant expression in his eyes. There was a great deal in that bronzed face, ruggedly handsome in an almost classical style with its crisp, dark hair, straight nose, and well-cut mouth, that might well have found favour, she was obliged to admit, with other members of her sex who had not been subjected to such a rude introduction to him; but she herself could at the moment feel only resentment towards its owner. While she stood debating with herself whether she ought to find a way to discover his identity and reveal to him her relationship to Jane (it would certainly make for an embarrassing meeting if she was first introduced to him as Jane's sister at some social gathering, in the presence of others), the stranger took matters into his own hands by remarking, obviously in response to her last ejaculation of, "A dozen years!" —"Yes. Does that surprise you? I seem to have tipped you a settler, somehow, with that remark!"

Gwendolen, having lived all her life under the same

roof with a father of definite sporting proclivities, could not but be perfectly familiar with boxing cant; but she was still too disturbed to put on a ladylike pretence of having not the least idea what the stranger had meant by "tipping her a settler," and, throwing caution to the winds, said that he had.

"You see," she said, "it told me who you were. Or should I say, who you are? At any rate," she went on, looking at him doubtfully, "I *think* it did—"

"I'm Lyndale, if that's of any help to you," the stranger offered.

He was regarding her with some curiosity now, she saw, as if he could not conceive in what way she might have become possessed of the knowledge of his intention to visit the neighbourhood; and it suddenly occurred to her that it could scarcely have entered his mind that the very dishevelled young lady standing before him, in a faded dimity frock and a squashed bonnet, was a relation of the beautiful and (thanks to Lady Priscilla's generosity) elegantly turned out Miss Jane Quarters whom he had known in London. To her intense annoyance, she found herself blushing like a schoolgirl.

"I'm—well, I daresay I ought to tell you, or it will seem very odd to you when you meet me, as I am sure you must!" she said rather disjointedly. "I am Jane's sister—"

"Jane's sister? Do you mean—Miss Jane Quarters?" It was now Lyndale's turn to look half puzzled, half incredulous, if that was the interpretation to be placed upon a sudden look of alertness in his blue eyes and the slight lifting of one dark eyebrow. "I see!" he said after a moment, without the least hint of discomposure. "Well, I *have* made a mull of it—haven't I? I gather you're not in-

clined to take kindly at the moment to having me in the family?"

"That," said Gwendolen, retreating into a primness quite foreign to her nature under the influence of her companion's outrageous frankness, "is not my affair, my lord. It is Jane's, and my father's."

"Yes, I daresay it is," Lyndale agreed. "But if I know females," he added (and Gwendolen had a sudden deep conviction that he did), "it's guineas to gooseberries you'll make it your affair, and do your best to paint me as black as Herod to your sister, only because I had the ill fortune to run you off the road."

"The thought," said Gwendolen rather tartly, for it seemed to her that she detected a notable lack of distress in his lordship's voice over the possibility that she might be able to influence Jane against him, "scarcely seems to disturb you, my lord!"

"Oh, it disturbs me, right enough!" Lyndale assured her. "A peaceful life is what I came to England for, Miss Quarters, and it wouldn't suit me in the least to find myself in the midst of tears and scenes. I'll tell you what," he offered, with an air of magnanimity, "let's go back and begin this all over again. You are walking along the lane, lost in thought; I come driving up at a sedate pace, become aware by some sixth sense that you are Miss Jane Quarters's sister, and halt my horses to enquire with the greatest civility whether I may take you up and deliver you at your front door —"

"Well, you mayn't!" Gwendolen interrupted him baldly. "I should be obliged to ask you to come in, and there is no one there to receive you — besides which, it is only cold beef and raspberries for nuncheon! You had much better go straight on to Beauworth, where I daresay you are expected."

"I daresay I am," his lordship said. "But I have an idea I'd find far better entertainment at — Brightleaves, is it? — than I shall at Beauworth. I've met my cousin, the Duke, only once, but he seems a tyrannical old file to me. What do you think of him yourself?"

Gwendolen considered. "It wouldn't be proper for me to say," she remarked at last, retiring into primness once more.

"Wouldn't it? Why not?"

"Because, my lord, we are not upon terms," Gwendolen was obliged to say, wondering how one could ever retain any decent reticences with a man who appeared totally incapable of abiding by the normal rules of polite conversation. She added hastily, seeing that he appeared on the point of saying, "Why not?" again, "The Duke wished to purchase Brightleaves several years ago, and he and Papa had words over it. They both have — very marked views, you see."

"Do they?" Lyndale appeared to consider this statement. "Does your father also have marked views about me?" he enquired after a moment, with an air of some interest.

"About *you?* Oh, no!" "If we must be frank," Gwendolen thought, casting prudence to the winds, "I suppose I had as well go the whole length." She went on to say, "I shouldn't think, actually, that he cares tuppence whom Jane marries, as long as he isn't what he calls a *scaly scrub*. And I expect even he will think it is rather splendid, your being a marquis."

"Do you?" Lyndale enquired.

"I?" Gwendolen, wondering rather wildly for a

moment if she was going to be led on by all this frank speaking to tell him about Alain de Combray, took herself firmly in hand, and after a moment said austerely that it made not the slightest degree of difference to her.

"Of course," she admitted, "it is otherwise with Mama. But then it always is with mothers—don't you agree? I daresay she might even be better pleased if the gentleman to whom *I* am betrothed were a marquis; but to my mind any title of that sort can never be so glorious as the title of captain, on active service, in His Majesty's Navy."

The appearance, round the bend in the lane, of a cart drawn by a small, obstinate-looking black horse, with a youth riding lazily on the shaft, interrupted the conversation at this point and caused Gwendolen to recollect the extreme impropriety of her standing there upon a public road in conversation with a gentleman to whom, although he might be going to marry her sister, she had after all not been properly introduced. She replied with great dignity to the youth's bashful greeting and said to the Marquis that she would now bid him good-day.

"Do you mean I really can't drive you to Brightleaves?" Lyndale demanded.

"No, you may not!" Gwendolen said. "It wouldn't be in the least *comme il faut*. But I should *love* to be taken up behind that splendid team, once we have been properly introduced!"

And she walked off down the lane.

"What in heaven's name," she asked herself as she got herself safely out of Lyndale's sight around the turn in the road, "will Jane say when she learns I have had this completely incredible conversation with her young man? And not so young, either, if it comes to that—thirty-three or —four, I should imagine. She can't possibly wish to marry him, of course. Dear, good, proper Jane—she would suffer agonies of embarrassment whenever she went into company with him, never knowing what he would do or say next! I do think Aunt Pris could have done better than this for her, marquis or no marquis! Of course, he *is* attractive—but not at all in the style Jane admires."

Lady Otilia had not yet returned when she reached the house, but Campaspe was there, having been driven from the Manor, after only a brief half hour with her beloved, by Lady Fairhall, who had the strictest ideas of propriety. Gwendolen at once dragged her upstairs to her bed-chamber and told the whole story of her meeting with Lyndale.

"He will never do for Jane," she said, shaking her head decidedly. "I daresay he would frighten her half out of her wits. Not that he doesn't appear quite a good-tempered sort of man—but still there is something extraordinary about him, as if he would do anything that came into his head if he felt like it. So I expect it will have to be Alain, after all."

Campaspe said, "Didn't I tell you so?"—and added that, if it *was* Alain, Mama would never forgive them.

"She was going on and *on*, all the way to the village, about how splendid it will be when Jane is a marchioness, and how of course Lyndale will do *something* to see to it that those dreadful moneylenders don't turn us all out of Brightleaves," she said. "She says he is fearfully rich. You know, Gwen," she continued, very earnestly for her, "things really *must* be in a frightful state when Mama begins worrying about them. All the same, Jane *can't* be expected to sell herself for Lyndale's gold—can she?"

Gwendolen said dampeningly not to be so melo-
dramatic.

Three

She was obliged to admit to herself, however, that it *was* a problem, and one that she was sure had occurred very forcibly to sensible, dutiful Jane, who knew just as well as Gwendolen that their father was quite incapable of managing Brightleaves in such a way as to put it upon a paying basis after the near-disaster of a few years back. All he had done with the considerable sum of money that Messrs. Smith and Brown had obligingly provided him with at that time had been to settle the most pressing debts; the rest had gone into the refurbishing of the stables and the acquisition of several new race horses.

Mr. Quarters, who had a very sanguine nature where horses were concerned, insisted that these were "investments" which, in the long run, would be far safer and more profitable than if he had placed the money in the Funds; but Gwendolen and Jane had more than once discussed the unlikelihood that such a happy outcome would occur, and there was every probability now, Gwendolen was inclined to think after her meeting with Lyndale, that if Jane were to accept the Marquis's suit, it would be only because she was aware that marriage with him would be the one practical means of preserving the entire family from ruin.

She was soon to have the opportunity of testing this theory, for shortly after nuncheon Lady Priscilla's travelling-chaise, bearing Jane herself under the chaperonage of Lady Priscilla's smart abigail, drew up before the front door of Brightleaves. Lady Otilia, who, since her return from her morning calls, had been awaiting this moment with great impatience, at once bore her daughter off to the drawing room, exclaiming as she did so upon the extraordinary improvement in her appearance that had taken place since her departure for London. Jane had left Gloucestershire, she declared, a beautiful young girl, but she had returned the young lady of fashion, complete in every modish detail.

And, indeed, the elegant little creature, in her China blue *pelissette* and ostrich-plumed bonnet of a matching colour, who now trod into the shabby drawing room looked a delicate exotic, as out of place there as an orchid in a bouquet of daisies.

Jane Quarters was indubitably a beautiful girl. Her eyes were azure blue, her ringletted hair a fashionable, dusky black, her features regular, but without the coldness of classical perfection, and her figure supple and exquisitely formed. Added to all this was an amiable disposition and an understanding quite sufficient to cope with the problems with which young ladies are ordinarily confronted; it was easy to see, Gwendolen thought, why

Lyndale, faced with no need to seek fortune in marriage and apparently bent only upon finding an attractive, conformable wife, had fixed his choice upon her. No doubt, she considered with a worldly wise knowledge based on her perusal of Lord Byron's more colourful descriptions of gentlemen who had led highly adventurous lives in exotic climes, men such as Lyndale, jaded with alluring Eastern houris, would savour the change to a normal, well-conducted English young lady such as Jane; but to see Jane sacrifice herself in such a marriage was beginning to seem quite as unthinkable to her as it already did to Campaspe.

Of course, Lady Otilia, unaware of the complexities of the situation, had no such scruples, and her very first remark to Jane, once she had done exclaiming over her improved appearance and had uttered a hasty and obviously perfunctory enquiry concerning Lady Priscilla's health, was, "And so, my dear, dear Jane, you are to be a marchioness! I scarcely dared hope, when I sent you off to London, for such a glorious outcome for my dreams for you! We have all been in transports since your aunt's letter arrived this morning — not your papa, of course, for he does not know of it as yet, having *most* vexingly gone to Cheltenham before the post came — but I am sure he will be as soon as he learns that Lyndale is to offer for you —"

Gwendolen, who had been watching her sister's face closely during this enthusiastic speech, saw the colour rise suddenly in Jane's cheeks and heard her utter a slight gasp.

"Oh!" she said rather faintly, after a moment. "It is — it is quite determined then, ma'am? I did not know — Aunt did not tell me, before I left London —"

"No, of course she did not, for she did not know it herself at the time," Lady Otilia said, quite oblivious to the agitation in her daughter's voice. "She sent an express off to me directly Lord Lyndale had spoken to her, which was just after you had set out on your journey. Lyndale is to come down to Beauworth without delay, she says; I daresay he will arrive in this part of the country within a day or two."

"He is here now," interjected Gwendolen, who had not previously described her meeting with Lyndale to her mother. Lady Otilia looked at her in some surprise. "We met quite by accident," Gwendolen added hastily, and went on to turn the subject as quickly as she could, which was not difficult, for Lady Otilia was far more interested in learning of Jane's activities in London than she was in hearing of her eldest daughter's meeting with Lord Lyndale.

It was almost dinnertime before Gwendolen and Campaspe could at last succeed in getting Jane to themselves. She had been reluctantly released by Lady Otilia so that she could change out of her travelling costume; but Gwendolen and Campaspe, waylaying her on the stairs, dragged her instead up to the old schoolroom at the top of the house and made her sit down upon a dilapidated sofa there.

"We want to *know*," Campaspe said, plumping herself down upon a stool directly opposite her sister and frowning at her portentously, her chin in her cupped hands and her elbows on her knees. "Do you *really* want to marry Lyndale? Aren't you in love with Alain anymore?"

To Campaspe's obvious satisfaction, this blunt interrogatory caused Jane to burst immediately into tears.

"There! Didn't I tell you?" Campaspe exclaimed, turning triumphantly to Gwendolen.

Gwendolen, however, with a reproving glance at her, sat down beside Jane upon the sofa and put her arms about her.

"There, there—don't cry, my dearest," she said soothingly. "If you don't wish to marry the man, you needn't, of course. After all, he hasn't even offered for you yet."

"But he w-will!" Jane sobbed. "Aunt s-said he would—only I d-didn't believe her, because he never showed the least s-sign of being in l-love with me—"

"Bless you, child, men like Lyndale needn't be in love with someone to offer marriage to her!" Gwendolen said practically. "They merely want a suitable wife, beautiful, if possible—and you *are* quite beautiful, unfortunately. If you were plain, now, you could marry Alain and no one would think twice about your throwing yourself away on a penniless Frenchman."

"No, I couldn't—marry Alain, that is," Jane said, drying her eyes determinedly as her sensible nature reasserted itself. "He hasn't any money—nor have I—and we should starve—"

"Fiddle!" said Campaspe briskly. "Papa hasn't any money, and we manage to live somehow. Though it *is* rather dreary to be poor," she added, looking round with disfavour at the forlorn schoolroom. "I've told Neil he *must* become a general soon, or at least a colonel, but he says it will be rather difficult now, since there isn't a war any longer. But I should marry him anyway," she declared defiantly, "even if he stayed a lieutenant for the rest of his life. And *you* must marry Alain, of course, Jane."

Jane shook her head, smoothing her handkerchief out upon her lap with great attention.

"No," she said after a moment, in a mournful voice. "I can never marry him. I must think of my duty."

"Your *duty?*" Campaspe stared at her. "Oh, Jane, *don't* be a ninnyhammer!" she said impatiently. "You sound like the heroine in one of those *revolting* novels where everyone is too dreadfully noble, except the ones who are terribly wicked—"

"But I *must* think of it," Jane persisted, tears welling up once more in her eyes. "I don't know how many times Aunt has told me that Mama has placed all her dependence upon my making an advantageous marriage—and you *see* how overjoyed she is, now that she thinks I am to marry Lord Lyndale! I couldn't *bear* to disappoint her—"

"Well, you must disappoint someone, certainly," Gwendolen said, "either her or Alain. You will have to choose which." And then, seeing the woebegone face Jane turned upon her, she went on, with a slight shrug, "Not that it appears to me that the choice should present the least difficulty. The matter might stand differently if you hadn't formed a lasting attachment for Alain—though I *do* think you would find being married to Lord Lyndale very uncomfortable, even if you weren't in love with someone else. But, as it is, you certainly cannot accept an offer from him, no matter how happy it would make Mama."

Jane shook her head once more. She had, as Gwendolen was well aware, a very persuadable nature, which made it ordinarily the easiest matter in the world to manage her; but there had always been a point, even when she had been a small girl, at which her better self

came into the picture, and then she could be quite maddeningly unreasonable, from the point of view of people
with the usual human imperfections. Gwendolen saw
with a sense of strong foreboding that she had the look of
confronting the scruples of that other self now.

"But I couldn't," she repeated in a gentle, earnest, obstinate voice. "I mean, I couldn't refuse Lord Lyndale,
and disappoint Mama so, and bring all of you to ruin,
when it is in my power to save you — "

"Stuff!" said Campaspe loudly. "*We* don't wish to be
saved — do we, Gwen? Not if it means you will be obliged
to marry a perfectly horrid man like Lord Lyndale."

Jane said pensively that he wasn't really *horrid*. "His
manners are a — a trifle abrupt, perhaps," she said. "But
Aunt says one becomes accustomed to a gentleman's little
peculiarities when one is married to him — "

"Well, *she* has never become accustomed to Uncle
Horace's 'little peculiarities,' " Gwendolen said frankly.
"They quarrel like a pair of monkeys, as you very well
know. But that is neither here nor there. The point is,
Cammie and I don't in the least wish you to sacrifice
yourself for *us*, because our husbands will do very well in
the world without Lord Lyndale's interest; and as for
Papa, I am sure he will say the same, if you tell him you
are in love with someone else — "

"But I *couldn't* do that!" said Jane, looking terrified at
the very thought. "You *know* what strong views he has
about the French! He would never consent to my
marrying Alain, even if Lord Lyndale were not to make
me an offer!"

Gwendolen and Campaspe gazed at each other in
silent exasperation. It was perfectly plain, their eyes said

eloquently, that Jane had got into one of her mud-dleheaded states, and that they would be obliged to rescue her from the disaster of a marriage with Lyndale without her lifting a hand to save herself.

"She really is the most nonsensical girl!" Gwendolen said, when she and Campaspe were alone together in the schoolroom, Jane having finally been permitted to go to her own bedchamber to change her frock. "If she were the romantic sort, it might be all very well for her to marry Lyndale, and moon about concealing a hopeless passion for Alain for years and years; I believe there *are* females who quite enjoy that kind of thing — at least, one reads about them in novels. But Jane is not romantic in the least. She is a respectable little creature, who would be perfectly horrified with herself if she found herself married and in love with a man who wasn't her husband. And she *is* in love with Alain still; it's as plain as a pikestaff. So what *are* we to do about her?"

Campaspe said rather doubtfully that they might tell Lord Lyndale that she was in love with someone else.

"Good heavens, no! We can't do *that!*" Gwendolen said, turning from one of the small windows that looked out to the west of the house, over the green-grey wold rip-pling off into the blue distance and the silver thread of the stream coveted by the Duke of Tardiff. "He might call Alain out."

"Oh! Do you really think so?" Campaspe, although not in the least a bloodthirsty girl, could not prevent an an-ticipatory gleam from appearing in her eyes at the prospect of so romantic an occurrence as a duel, especially since she saw it in her imagination as a quite outmoded conflict with flashing, thrusting swords, instead of the deadlier but far less picturesque modern combat with firearms. "Do you really think he would be likely to do that?" she demanded.

"I haven't the least notion *what* he would be likely to do," Gwendolen said, "except that it would be something that no one expected, and probably *quite* upsetting. So I don't think we ought to bring Alain into this. We shall simply have to manage it ourselves, because Jane won't, and Mama won't, and Papa—" She broke off suddenly, looking thoughtful. "Papa—" she repeated slowly, and then added, with a dreamy upward glance that gave her an angelically innocent appearance but would have deceived no one who knew her well, "after all, Lyndale *is* the Duke's cousin, you know. I *don't* think Papa would take kindly to *that* connexion."

Campaspe flew at her and gave her an enthusiastic hug. "Of course—the very thing!" she exclaimed. "If we keep harping on *that*, he is bound to get up on his high ropes and say Jane can't marry Lyndale! You *are* clever, Gwen!"

But they were reckoning without their papa's ruling passion. Mr. Quarters, coming in just at dinnertime from a most satisfactory day in Cheltenham, where he had concluded what he appeared to consider a highly advantageous bargain involving the sale of one horse, the purchase of two others, and an arrangement to have a stallion with a stupendous pedigree become the (at least prospective) father of a gifted colt or filly by Mr. Quarters's favourite mare—all of which matters he discussed with the greatest freedom before his daughters—evidently felt the subject of Jane's forthcoming betrothal to be an affair of secondary importance when it was first broached to him over the neat's tongue and cauliflowers.

"Lyndale? I don't know any Lyndale," he said summarily, as if that disposed of the topic. And, when Lady Otilia persisted, "A marquis, eh?" he said. "I've never held with marquisates: a jumped-up sort of title. Earls and barons were good enough for us in the old days."

Mr. Quarters was a tall, bony man, with the lean, rufous face and piercing blue eyes of the born enthusiast. He was, in his way, a good-humoured man when not crossed, and had always been much in favour with the eldest and youngest of his daughters; but Jane, like Lady Otilia, felt about him much as her superstitious Stone Age ancestors might have felt about the unpredictable forces of Nature—as an entity sometimes benignant, sometimes terrifying, but always totally incomprehensible.

Lady Otilia, however, had long since learned that even forces of Nature, if attacked perseveringly enough when it was worth one's while, and philosophically ignored when it was not, could be coped with. She went on talking quite calmly about Lyndale's sterling qualifications to be accepted into the Quarters family, among the most noteworthy of which were, naturally, his estates in Derbyshire and Kent and his income of fifty thousand a year.

"And as to family," Gwendolen, who had been awaiting her opportunity, casually interjected after a time, "you know, of course, Papa, that he is cousin to the Duke of Tardiff."

Mr. Quarters's knife and fork were laid down abruptly; the bushy, reddish brows drew together to shadow the penetrating glare of his blue eyes in a manner that always terrified Jane.

35

"What's that you say?" he barked. "The Duke of Tardiff?"

"Yes, Papa," said Gwendolen demurely, casting a significant glance at Campaspe, who could scarcely conceal her satisfaction as she waited for the explosion to come.

Mr. Quarters's hand struck the table with a blow that set the dishes jumping.

"Now, by Jupiter!" he ejaculated. "By—Jupiter! If that isn't the most amazing piece of luck!"

"*Luck*, Papa!" Campaspe stared at him incredulously. "But didn't you hear what Gwen said? He is cousin to the Duke!"

"The devil fly away with the Duke!" Mr. Quarters said impatiently but without animus, as if he were too elated to trouble himself over his old enemy. "Don't you understand, girl? *This* is the man who is said to have induced the Sultan of Morocco to part with a pair of pure-bred Arabian mares—*mares*, by God!—you know the Arabs hold them sacred—and has brought them back with him to England! There hasn't been such a *coup* since the Darley Arabian was picked up in Syria! By God, I shall look forward to meeting him!"

Campaspe and Gwendolen gazed at each other in despair; Jane looked bewildered; and Lady Otilia, signalling with a dreamy air for the pudding to be brought in, said complacently that she fancied he might have that pleasure very soon. She then began discussing with Jane which of the gowns she had brought back with her from London would do for Campaspe when they were invited, as she was sure they must be, to dine at Beauworth.

Four

On the following morning Lady Otilia, eager to display to the world the exquisitely fashionable new Jane who had returned to her from London, persuaded her to accompany her on a walk to the village to make some trifling purchases—an excursion that was quite likely to end, Gwendolen was well aware, in a call at the Rectory or the Manor, even if the Rutledges, who lived in a handsome red brick house fronting upon the High Street, did not observe them from their drawing-room windows and beckon them to come in.

Gwendolen herself, having planned to spend the morning over the household accounts, was thankful for this excuse not to join the party; but Campaspe, who had constituted herself a sort of watchdog for Jane, as if she felt that her presence beside her would at least have the power to prevent Lyndale from making an immediate attempt to carry her off, readily accepted Lady Otilia's invitation to accompany her and Jane. There was no danger, Lady Otilia announced, that Lord Lyndale would call upon his important errand before they returned, for gentlemen of fashion never rose before noon, and by the hour at which they might reasonably expect him they would have long concluded their errands and be back at Brightleaves.

Alas! Lady Otilia had reckoned without that knowledge of Lord Lyndale's character which had caused Gwendolen to declare to Campaspe that, whatever he did, it would be something that no one expected and probably quite upsetting. She, Gwendolen, was still in the morning room, wrestling with the accounts, and the village party had not yet returned, when the housekeeper appeared in the doorway to announce that Lord Lyndale had arrived.

"Bother!" exclaimed Gwendolen, who had not the lease desire to entertain Lyndale tête-à-tête, and, in fact, would have gone to considerable lengths to be able to escape meeting him at all. She stood up, glancing down resignedly at her plain round gown and ink-stained fingers; it did not require a mirror to tell her that her hair was rather untidy as well. No doubt Lyndale must be convinced when he saw her that she never presented the least appearance of *à la modality*. "Is my father in the stables, Pratson?" she went on, to the housekeeper. "Send someone at once to fetch him, please, and show Lord Lyndale into the drawing room."

As Pratson left the morning room, Gwendolen rapidly smoothed her curls and straightened her collar, thinking as she did so, "Since I *must* see him, I wonder if I ought to take advantage of the opportunity to do what I can to rescue Jane? I *can't* simply tell him she is in love with someone else, but perhaps if I could drop a hint to him that it might be well to take the matter slowly, until Jane has time to become better acquainted with him? That would at least give her time to know her own mind better than she seems to do at present!"

How his lordship would receive such a hint from her she could not guess, but he could do no more, at any rate, she thought, than give her a set-down for her attempt to interfere in his affairs.

It was in this frame of mind that she walked into the drawing room, and, in the determination to do nothing to set his lordship's back up before she had even begun to put her plan into action, trod across the carpet towards him with her hand out and a smile upon her lips.

"Good morning!" she said. "I am afraid Jane is out at the moment, but she is expected back soon, and Papa is only gone out to the stables and will be here directly. Won't you—?" She had been about to invite him to sit down, but the words died on her lips as she saw the smile of amusement that had suddenly appeared upon his lordship's bronzed face. "What is the matter?" she demanded, wondering with a horrid sense of self-consciousness if she had got ink on the tip of her nose, or something equally ridiculous. "Why are you looking at me in that—that *odious* way?"

"What 'odious way'?" Lyndale countered. He had a very strong hand-clasp, and she found it impossible to draw her own hand away from his immediately, as she had intended. "If you mean my natural expression of surprise over this unexpectedly cordial greeting—"

"You aren't surprised; you're amused!" Gwendolen said down-rightly. "And why shouldn't I be cordial? I have *some* notion of conduct, my lord, whatever the — the *disagreeable* circumstances of our last meeting may have been!"

"Very commendable, I'm sure!" Lyndale said gravely, but still with the same glint of amusement in his very blue eyes. "It's refreshing to meet a young lady with such a forgiving nature! Were you about to ask me to sit down? Thank you; I shall be happy to."

And he suited the action to the words. Gwendolen perforce sat down as well, and confronted him across the comfortable, shabby drawing room with as much self-composure as she could summon up. The most exasperating thing about Lord Lyndale, she was telling herself with some indignation, was that he seemed always capable of setting one on end before one had been three minutes in his company.

However, she had not in the least forgotten her resolution to do something to postpone his fixing Jane hard and fast to a betrothal before she — Jane — had had time to resolve the conflict between love and duty that was so much disturbing her at present, and, cutting ruthlessly through the civil observation Lyndale had begun to make about the fine weather they were having, said to him abruptly, "Lord Lyndale — "

"Yes?" said Lyndale encouragingly, as, after having taken the initial plunge, she hesitated, not knowing quite how to begin.

"I — I should like to speak to you about Jane!" Gwendolen said, wondering what there was about Lyndale's polite but rather skeptically attentive gaze that made it so extraordinarily difficult to converse with him with one's usual aplomb. "She is — she is very young!" she plunged on rather desperately, as he gave no sign of intending to say anything himself. "*Very* young!" she repeated even more desperately, having not the least notion how she was to go on from there.

"Very," agreed Lyndale equably. "You, I daresay, Miss Quarters, are much older, now?"

"Well, no—not *much* older," Gwendolen said a trifle indignantly, wondering if he considered her quite "old-cattish." "Two years. But that makes a *great* deal of difference, you know!"

"A great deal of difference about what?" enquired Lyndale, looking willing to be informed.

Gwendolen cast her last ounce of reticence to the winds. "About being married, of course!" she said.

"I see." To her relief, Lyndale did not appear at all put out by this bald announcement; on the contrary, he went on, in a quite ordinary, conversational tone, "I take it, Miss Quarters, that you consider yourself of a ripe age to undertake matrimony, then; in fact, if I remember correctly, I believe you informed me yesterday that you are actually engaged at present to marry a captain in the Royal Navy?"

"Captain Henry Belville—yes!" said Gwendolen, with some degree of pride. "He will be arriving here tomorrow; I have had a letter from him only this morning. So you will no doubt have an opportunity to meet him—"

"Belville?" One of Lyndale's mobile dark brows went up. "But I already know Captain Belville," he remarked surprisingly. "I don't imagine there can be two of them in the Royal Navy—God help the Navy if there are!—so this must be the man—"

"What do you mean—'God help the Navy'?" Gwendolen demanded, bristling. "Captain Belville is one of the heroes of our late wars, Lord Lyndale! He served under Nelson!"

"Yes, I know," said Lyndale. "And Lord Nelson has all my sympathy. Of all the pompous, opinionated asses—! Surely, Miss Quarters, you aren't seriously proposing to marry that fellow!"

For a moment Gwendolen was so overcome with astonishment and wrath that she could scarcely speak.

"I most certainly am!" she declared roundly, when she had recovered herself sufficiently to utter the words. "And, what is more, I shall consider myself honoured to do so, sir!"

Lyndale shook his head incredulously. "I don't believe it!" he declared. "You can't be well acquainted with him—or he with you—or he would never have offered marriage to you, or you have accepted him!"

Gwendolen assured him austerely that her acquaintance with Captain Belville dated back more than two years, but basely omitted to add that that acquaintance had consisted of nothing more than having sat beside him twice at dinner parties, stood up to dance with him once at the Cheltenham Assembly, and enjoyed a ten-minute tête-à-tête with him in the Rutledges' drawing room, during the course of which she had got over her awe of him sufficiently to inform him in a very breathless voice how happy she would be if he would honour her with an occasional letter from his post of duty, describing the arduous excitements of his life at sea.

The letters had gradually become more frequent as the months had gone by, owing chiefly to her habit of replying to the Captain's missives on the same day that she received them; and before a year was out, it had somehow become an established fact that there was an "understanding" between them, which had eventually progressed to an engagement proper, followed (to make it quite official) by an announcement in the *Morning Post*. Mrs. Rutledge's belief that Gwendolen had "managed" the whole affair of the engagement was therefore unwarranted, although it was probably true that there never would have been an engagement if she had not written such long, enthusiastic letters to Captain Belville, who was not ordinarily a man to be swept off his feet by a girl without a fortune. But every man, even a naval hero, has his Achilles' heel, and in Captain Belville's case it was his uneasy conviction that a gentleman could not properly carry on a voluminous correspondence with a young lady to whom he was not betrothed.

Gwendolen's assurances as to the length of her acquaintance with Captain Belville did not appear to alter Lyndale's conviction that she and the Captain had made a signal error by becoming betrothed to each other, but she did not allow him to expatiate further on the subject.

"We were discussing," she reminded him inexorably, keeping her indignation well under for the sake of her purpose, "Jane's being married, not my own situation, my lord. Let us return to that subject, if you please, for there is something I should like to say to you before my father comes in."

"By all means," Lyndale agreed politely. "You were remarking, I believe, that your sister is very young, and that you, on the other hand, are much—I beg your pardon!—*two years* older. Now where do we go on from there?"

It was exactly like him, she thought wrathfully, as he

sat gazing at her with a civilly expectant expression upon his face, not to make the least push to help her, when he *must* know what she wished to say to him. But there was nothing for it but to come out with it now, so she said, with as aloof an air as she found it possible to assume under the circumstances, "I merely wished to remind you, my lord, that it may be wise for you to—to proceed slowly in a matter of such importance as matrimony with a girl of Jane's age and—and timid disposition," she added inspirationally, and then looked at him hopefully to see if he had now quite taken her meaning.

As usual, she found he had not only taken it, but was willing to put it into words in the bluntest of terms.

"I see," he remarked. "Still, you can hardly expect me to shab off, can you, Miss Quarters?—when I've made it rather publicly known that I've come to Gloucestershire for the express purpose of offering for your sister? I shall make my offer, of course—and if, as you seem to be trying to tell me, she finds that offer unacceptable, she will have every opportunity to let me know of it."

"Oh, but I didn't—I don't mean—" Gwendolen interrupted him hastily, hearing her father's footsteps in the hall and suddenly aghast at the conviction that she had taken far too much upon herself. After all, Jane herself had not said that she wished the projected match to be abandoned, and certainly both Gwendolen's mother and her father, to say nothing of Lady Priscilla, would be severely displeased if they knew she had done anything to throw a rub in the way of it.

It was too late for her to say more, however, for at that moment Mr. Quarters walked into the room, wearing his usual outdoors costume of a cutty green coat, a pair of old drab breeches, and antiquated top-boots.

"Good morning to you, my lord, and welcome to Brightleaves," he said, advancing towards Lyndale with his hand outstretched and an eager expression upon his face. "Now about those mares—"

Gwendolen, seeing very well what sort of turn the conversation was about to take, gave it up and, excusing herself almost immediately, went back to the morning room and her accounts.

It was useless to pretend to herself that her brief conversation with Lyndale had not left her in a state of considerable discomposure. In the first place, she was exceedingly angry with him because of the astounding and most discourteous remarks he had made about Captain Belville, and in the second place, she had an uncomfortable feeling that everyone else in the family—except, of course, Campaspe—was going to be exceedingly angry with *her* if they were to find out about the imprudent remarks she had made to him on the subject of Jane. Marquises, after all, did not grow on trees, particularly marquises with fortunes of fifty thousand a year; and her family, she felt, would have every right to censure her severely if Jane, forced by hard circumstance to give up all thoughts of marrying Alain de Combray, was obliged in the end to wed a husband far less desirable from a worldly point of view than Lyndale.

She was somewhat consoled about her rashness, however, when, her mother and sisters arriving home soon afterwards from their excursion to the village, Campaspe stopped in the morning room to tell her that they had chanced to come up on Alain de Combray in the High Street, and that his agitation, and Jane's, over this unexpected encounter had been plain to anyone who wasn't as blind as a beetle.

"It was the saddest thing I ever saw in my life," she declared with much dramatic emphasis, "exactly like the scene in *The Betrayed Lovers* where Maximilian meets Ermentrude for the last time and he only presses her hand and goes away without speaking because he is too overcome with grief to utter a word. Only Alain couldn't press Jane's hand, of course, because he was carrying half a dozen packages he had purchased for the Duke, and he *did* say *Good morning*, but hardly anything more. I could see that he knew all about Lyndale—well, he *would*, of course, since Lyndale is staying at Beauworth. And Jane had tears in her eyes—"

All this made Gwendolen feel that perhaps she had not been so very wicked, after all, to hint to Lyndale that Jane might not be overwhelmed with joy over his proposal. And when she had confided her misdeed to Campaspe, and had heard from her how Jane had gone white as a sheet on being informed by Pratson that Lyndale was even then in the house and being commanded by Lady Otilia to run upstairs and tidy her hair before she made her appearance in the drawing room, she began to feel almost virtuous again.

"Poor Jane!" she and Campaspe said to each other; and then they both hoped aloud that their sister would not be such a widgeon as to accept Lyndale's offer if she didn't wish to.

"I wonder if Mama will leave her alone with him?" Campaspe debated. "She has such strict ideas of propriety—that is, when she remembers them."

Gwendolen said that, in her opinion, it was their papa who would not leave them alone, not because he had any ideas of propriety at all, but because he would not wish to stop talking about horses to Lyndale.

But as it fell out, Lady Otilia, with a marquis and fifty thousand pounds a year at stake, was for once a match for her husband's horse-mania, and by dint of several broad hints and a final outflanking action which included actually taking him by the arm and leading him out of the room, succeeded in giving Lyndale the opportunity for a private conversation with Jane. She had also, she stated with some smugness to Gwendolen and Campaspe as they waited in deep suspense for this conversation to be concluded, managed to pin her spouse down to the subject of Jane long enough for him to assure Lyndale that he had no objection to the Marquis's paying his addresses to her, so that there was now no obstacle, she remarked complacently, between her middle daughter and a coronet.

Unfortunately for her hopes, the matter turned out to be not quite so simple as that. Lyndale, emerging from the drawing room, not ten minutes after she had left him alone with Jane, with a rather thoughtful air which even Lady Otilia could not translate as the mien of a triumphant lover, merely informed her courteously, before taking himself off, that he fancied it might be best for her to hear from Jane herself how matters stood — an ominous statement that sent Lady Otilia into the drawing room with the gravest misgivings the moment the front door had closed behind him.

Gwendolen and Campaspe followed her. They found Jane seated on the sofa, dissolved in gentle tears. She looked up mistily as Lady Otilia entered.

"Oh, Mama!" she said, with a wavering attempt at a smile. "Lord Lyndale has been so kind — so very considerate! I should not have believed —"

"Kind? Considerate?" Lady Otilia's misgivings appeared to deepen: young ladies, her face suggested, who had just received an offer of marriage and had returned a blushing affirmative answer did not ordinarily use such terms in describing their prospective bridegroom's behaviour. "What had he to be kind and considerate about?" she demanded. The colour came up abruptly beneath the perfect alabaster of Jane's complexion. "Surely," said Lady Otilia awfully, sensing the worst, "you did not Refuse Him, Jane!"

"Oh, no—no, Mama!" Jane said quickly and distressfully.

"Thank God!" Lady Otilia sank into an armchair, where she reclined with one hand pressed over her heart. "I do not believe," she said dramatically, "that I could have survived such a disappointment—"

"It is only, Mama," Jane went on, regarding her with anxious timidity, "not quite—quite *settled* yet, you see. That is to say, Lord Lyndale has told me that, though he wishes very much to marry me, he does not wish *me* to feel bound to give him any—any really binding promise until I am *quite* ready to, so that in the meantime we may go on comfortably and learn to know each other better—"

"I have never heard of such nonsense!" declared Lady Otilia, bouncing up to sit erect in her chair with an energy that quite belied her languid manner of a moment before. "Learn to know each other better! Pray, what is there for you to know about *him* but that he is a gentleman of title, fortune, and unexceptionable character" (Gwendolen blinked, recalling certain not-so-veiled-hints about the Marquis's adventures abroad that had penetrated even to Gloucestershire) "or for him to know about *you* but that you are a young lady of ex-

48

cellent birth, modest habits, and a proper education? Do you mean to tell me, you ridiculous girl, that you have left matters so? — that you are not now actually engaged to him?"

"Well," said Jane doubtfully, "I don't really know that, dearest Mama. That is, he says he considers himself engaged to *me*, but that I am not to consider myself engaged to *him* unless I am sure I wish to be. That *does* seem rather odd, I expect, but it sounded *quite* sensible when he was proposing it to me, and made me feel so very much more comfortable — "

Lady Otilia, calling upon heaven to be her witness that she had never done anything in a blameless life to deserve having such a peagoose for a daughter, again sank back against the cushions of her armchair, evidently somewhat mollified, however, by the fact that the accomplishment of a proper engagement obviously waited only upon her success in overcoming Jane's unaccountable scruples against it.

Meanwhile, Gwendolen realised with astonishment that her conversation with Lyndale, unsatisfactory as it had seemed at the time, had apparently borne fruit in the way of an arrangement which she felt even she could not have improved upon. There would be ample time now for Jane to decide whether or not she really wished to give up the prospect of becoming a marchioness for what seemed a hopeless attachment to Alain de Combray; and, in the meantime, there was Lyndale to be had for the lifting of a finger.

All rather too good to be true, Gwendolen found herself thinking suspiciously, for she could not bring herself to believe, after her own unfortunate experiences with his lordship, that magnanimity and a willingness to be led by

49

a female formed any large part of his character. No doubt, she thought, he had had his own selfish reasons for behaving towards Jane as he had done, so that there was no necessity for her to modify her disapproval of him — now intensified a hundredfold by his rude and quite uncalled for remarks about Captain Belville — by giving him credit, as Jane was doing, for "kindness" and "consideration."

But at this point the train of her thoughts, and of those of her mother and sisters, was abruptly altered by the arrival of one of the Duke of Tardiff's undergrooms, bearing a note from the Duke's unmarried daughter, Lady Maria Boulting, who served as his hostess, inviting the family at Brightleaves to dine at Beauworth on the Friday. *Not* a large party, the note stated in almost apologetic terms — for Lady Maria, unlike her irascible papa, was timid and self-effacing to a fault — but merely a conversable evening, with a few friends.

Lady Otilia's eyes gleamed as she perused the note, and a look of determination crept into her plump, pretty face. Mr. Quarters, the look said, might do as he pleased about accepting Lady Maria's invitation — and, knowing her husband, Lady Otilia was quite sure that what he pleased would be *not* to go to Beauworth. But wild horses, that look went on to say, would not prevent *her* from taking her daughters there, and attired, moreover, in the first stare of fashion, if another mortgage had to be taken out on Brightleaves in order to allow her to do so.

Five

However, no such drastic measures turned out to be necessary, owing largely to Lady Priscilla's forethought. Lady Priscilla, quite as aware as her sister that Jane's new position in Society as the betrothed of the Marquis of Lyndale would place a perilous strain upon the wardrobes of the ladies at Brightleaves, had been beforehand in making provision for this emergency. Thus, in addition to providing Jane with gowns suitable for every social occasion she might meet with during her London Season (some of which might well be pressed into service now for Campaspe, who was much the same size and height as Jane), she had also sent in the chaise with Jane some of her own frocks, not as yet in the least *démodé*, though her ladyship had tired of wearing them.

Lady Priscilla, like Gwendolen, was tall, slender, and fair; she had excellent taste and a penchant for youthful fashions, and Lady Otilia, going through the gowns she had sent with an eye to the Beauworth party, found what she considered the perfect dress for her eldest daughter to wear upon that occasion. It was a gown of almond-green crape, cut low across the bosom, the skirt front quite smooth and flat, with fulness concentrated in pleats at the back, and the hem finished with an embroidered band. As Lady Otilia complacently observed, it shrieked of a Bruton Street modiste's elegant atelier, and even Gwendolen, whose taste did not often agree with her mama's more exotic notions of fashion, gave it her unqualified approval.

Rather than considering its effect upon the ducal party at Beauworth, however, *her* mind was dwelling, as she regarded her reflection in her dressing-table mirror on the morning following Lyndale's visit to Brightleaves, upon the impression it might make upon Captain Henry Belville when, as would certainly occur now that he was at last to return to Gloucestershire, she and he would be fellow guests at such festive occasions as dinner-parties and balls. She was a trifle nervous, she found, about her forthcoming reunion with the gallant Captain, not being at all certain either how she should conduct herself on their first meeting or how he would conduct himself. They had been comparative strangers, after all, when they had last seen each other; yet now they were engaged to become man and wife. Would he clasp her to his manly bosom when they met? Somehow she could not imagine his doing that. On the other hand, she thought, they could hardly shake hands and say, "How do you do?" as mere acquaintances might.

The worst thing of all, it seemed to Gwendolen, as she looked forward doubtfully to their forthcoming meeting, was her remembrance of Lyndale's derogatory description of Captain Belville — "Of all the pompous, opinionated asses —!" Of course, she knew one really should not dignify such an obviously prejudiced remark by giving it even temporary room in one's memory; but, vexingly, she found she could not banish it from her mind. Naturally, she was quite aware that what the odious Marquis spoke of as pomposity was merely the innate dignity conferred upon a man's behaviour by a noble mind, and that when he had so meanly characterised Captain Belville as opinionated, he had merely been giving vent to an ordinary man's envy of a breadth of knowledge that made its possessor capable of providing the correct answer to any question that might be brought up in conversation.

All the same, the remark seemed to have watered and cultivated some nagging seed of doubt in her mind that had lain comfortably dormant there for the past two years; and it had grown into quite a monstrous little weed, exuding apprehension from every prickly leaf by the time she, her mother, and sisters set out for the Rutledges' on the morning following his lordship's visit.

Whether she was destined to meet her betrothed at the Rutledges', she was not at all certain. Captain Belville, in the letter of which she had spoken to Lyndale on the previous day, had informed her merely that he hoped to be in Gloucestershire on this date, but without specifying any time of arrival, and had added that, as the Rutledges had invited him to be their guest, he need not trespass upon the hospitality of Brightleaves.

This arrangement, even in view of the Captain's relationship to the Rutledges, had struck Gwendolen as slightly peculiar, and to Lady Otilia, with her maternal sensitivity to anything that appeared in the least degree likely to interfere with her present blissful condition of having three daughters all engaged to be married at one and the same time, it had immediately taken on a sinister aspect.

"Depend upon it," she had said impressively to Gwendolen, "Annabel Rutledge has not given up hope that she may yet detach Belville from you and see him marry Evelina instead. I have no doubt that is what is behind this scheme of hers to have him stay with *them* instead of with *us*. But never fear, my love! *I* shall see that nothing of the sort occurs!"

And in pursuit of her plan to scotch any machinations that Mrs. Rutledge might have in mind, Lady Otilia announced her intention of calling at the Rutledges' that every morning, with the purpose of discovering precisely when Captain Belville was expected there.

Gwendolen herself, invited—or, rather, commanded—to accompany her, was torn between dignity and curiosity; but, as duty certainly came down upon the latter side, she pocketed her pride and went with her mother, with Campaspe and Jane rounding out the party. Perhaps rather too large a delegation, Gwendolen felt uneasily, but uneasiness was swallowed up in disagreeable astonishment when, upon their being admitted to the house by the Rutledges' butler, they found Captain Belville himself seated comfortably in the drawing room, being entertained by Mrs. Rutledge and Evelina.

Lady Otilia, never one to allow a dramatic situation to escape her, checked upon the threshold and eyed him with what Campaspe later irreverently described as her Lady Macbeth look.

"Hah! Belville!" she said.

The Captain started nervously and rose from his chair with an alacrity ordinarily quite foreign to his demeanour. He was a tall, high-shouldered man, with a long face, a rather severe manner, and was seldom known to smile. A somewhat unhappy smile, however, had indubitably appeared upon his lips as the Quarters contingent entered the room, and he stammered, with a notable lack of that aplomb which, to an adoring younger Gwendolen, had made him appear the epitome of the British naval man, "Lady Otilia! Miss Quarters! What a surprise! What a — a very *pleasant* surprise!"

"Yes, it is — isn't it?" said Lady Otilia, regarding him without the least attempt to hide the suspicion that was obviously burning in her bosom. "A surprise, I mean, but not an entirely agreeable surprise to *me*, Captain Belville, to find you arrived in our midst while *we* remain quite in ignorance of your presence here! Annabel," — she turned to Mrs. Rutledge with an air of strong reproof — "I am astonished — nay, more than astonished: amazed! — that you did not send us word immediately of Belville's arrival!"

Mrs. Rutledge, a fair, plump, voluble woman who was ordinarily quite subservient in her manner towards Lady Otilia because, having married above her station, she appreciated the patronage of an earl's daughter, shrugged her shoulders a trifle recalcitrantly.

"Dear Lady Otilia," she cried vivaciously, "of course I was *just* about to sit down and write you a note telling you of Henry's arrival when you walked into the room! Naturally there was no point in disturbing you last evening —"

"Last evening!" Lady Otilia ruffled up even more and

regarded Captain Belville so severely that he might have been pardoned for quailing before her almost as visibly as a midshipman before the stern gaze of Lord Nelson himself. "Am I to understand then, Belville," she addressed him directly, "that you arrived here *last evening* and have not yet found an opportunity of waiting upon us at Brightleaves—?"

"Oh, Mama, for heaven's sake! There is no need to make a song about it!" interrupted Gwendolen, who had had quite enough of this embarrassing scene. She advanced upon Captain Belville and, extending her hand, said to him briskly, "How nice to see you again, Captain Belville! Did you have a pleasant journey from Portsmouth?"

It was not at all the sort of greeting she had thought to give her betrothed, but she saw at once that she had said exactly the right thing, for the Captain, quite out of his depth in the face of Lady Otilia's histrionics, immediately seized upon these commonplace remarks and in reply embarked upon a sea of commonplaces of his own. The company was treated to a detailed account of the deplorable condition of the post-chaise in which he had travelled from Portsmouth, the insolence of one of the post-boys, and the complete inadequacy of the dinner to which he had been obliged to sit down at the George in Cheltenham—"not wishing to give Cousin Annabel the trouble of an unexpected guest at *her* table," he explained, which statement caused Mrs. Rutledge to burst into the conversation again with a paean of admiration for his consideration, coupled with an appeal to Evelina to confirm her boast that she kept a table such that, if obliged to increase her covers even for half a dozen guests, it would have placed no strain upon her resources.

"For you *know* there has never been anything in the least clutchfisted about Mr. Rutledge," she said, smiling upon Captain Belville with such a proprietary expression that Lady Otilia, who had permitted herself to sit down, although with an air of in no wise sanctioning the conversation, considered most uncalled for. "Never the least word of complaint from him over the household expenses, no matter how much the butcher's bill may come to—but, there! he can afford it, and his opinion is *quite* the same as mine, that people who can live comfortably ought to do so. When all is said and done, there is only the one chick for it all to go to when we are gone."

And she smiled maternally upon Evelina, who blushed, looked at Captain Belville, and then dropped her eyelids in what Lady Otilia considered a most provocative manner.

All in all, as Lady Otilia told her highly uninterested husband later in the day in an outraged voice, it was the most vulgarly obvious *lure* she had ever heard in her life—"and before Gwendolen, too! As if Annabel Rutledge, and Evelina, too, didn't know perfectly well that she is engaged to him!"

Mr. Quarters, who was reading the *Racing Chronicle*, said without lifting his eyes from that journal that perhaps the Rutledges felt that engagements entered into by correspondence were not as binding as the ordinary kind.

"Nonsense!" said Lady Otilia roundly. "I know you have never liked Captain Belville above half, Mr. Quarters, but let me remind you that, whether you like him or not, he has engaged himself to marry one of your daughters, and it is *your* duty to see that he lives up to the obligation! It is a great pity that you weren't in when he walked back to Brightleaves with us this morning, as you might otherwise well have taken the opportunity *then* to put him in mind of that."

This time Mr. Quarters's eyes were raised for a fraction of a second from the *Chronicle* as he remarked, in a tone of considerable scorn, that there was no need for anything of *that* sort.

"That fellow Belville," he said, "hasn't the rumgumption to throw a girl over. Might make a scandal, and he wouldn't care for that. Good God, no! Careful as an old woman of his reputation."

Lady Otilia, who, in spite of displaying an unexpectedly practical side in regard to the business of marrying off her daughters, much preferred to keep matters upon a more romantic plane, said rather crossly that she believed Captain Belville to be much attached to Gwendolen and she to him, but that people like Annabel Rutledge could always cause trouble, even between true lovers, and so she had asked Captain Belville to dinner, *sans* the Rutledges, for the following day.

But as this interesting piece of information, involving as it did a decided snub to her most intimate friend, was received by Mr. Quarters with no more than a snort, signifying impatience at her continued interruption of his reading, the conversation perforce came to an end upon this unsatisfactory note.

Meanwhile, Gwendolen, who was pretending to be writing letters in the morning room, chiefly so that she could escape from all conversations involving affairs of the heart, which appeared to be the only topic that interested the female contingent at Brightleaves, sat nibbling at the tip of her pen while she reviewed the events of the morning, and particularly of that part of the morning between the departure of the Quarters ladies from the Rutledges' and their arrival at Brightleaves.

They had been accompanied, at Lady Otilia's rather pointed suggestion, by Captain Belville; and Gwendolen had no doubt that it was likewise by her mother's contrivance that she and the Captain had found themselves walking side by side ahead of the others, while Lady Otilia lagged unaccountably far behind with Jane and Campaspe.

A tête-à-tête of reasonable length had thus been made possible to the long-separated lovers, which Lady Otilia had no doubt expected would overcome the disagreeable effect of that uncomfortable reunion in the Rutledges' drawing room. But, unfortunately, such had not been the case. The conversation, in fact, as Gwendolen reviewed it now in her mind, had gone, as far as she could recall it, something like this:

BELVILLE. What very agreeable weather we are having, Miss Quarters! Don't you find it so? Or perhaps you would prefer it to be not quite so warm?

GWENDOLEN. I expect you ought to call me Gwendolen now. It's a rather silly name, but then Mama has a very romantic nature, you see. And, after all, it is not as bad as Campaspe.

BELVILLE (*nervously*) Of course. Of course, my—my dear Gwendolen!

GWENDOLEN. And shall I call you Henry?

BELVILLE (*bringing up a smile but still very nervous*) Naturally—naturally! It would be entirely suitable. (*Continuing with rather an air of misery seeking company*) I understand from my cousin Annabel that both your sisters are to be married soon as well?

GWENDOLEN. Well, not *exactly*. That is, of course Cammie is engaged to Neil Fairhall, but Jane hasn't actually accepted Lord Lyndale's offer.

BELVILLE (*surprised, almost incredulous*) Hasn't accepted—? But, my dear Miss—my dear Gwendolen, you cannot mean that she is considering refusing such an extremely advantageous offer! It seems quite—unthinkable!

GWENDOLEN. Well, it certainly isn't unthinkable, but I don't expect it is very likely, either. (*With a speculative glance at him*) I believe you are acquainted with Lord Lyndale, Henry. Do *you* think he is a suitable husband for Jane?

BELVILLE (*somewhat taken aback*) Suitable? I don't quite understand—He has a handsome fortune, I believe, now that he has come into the title—

GWENDOLEN. Oh, very handsome! But that is not at all what I mean.

BELVILLE. Naturally, matters would be vastly different if he had not inherited! Were he the penniless adventurer whom I had the misfortune to come across during my service in the Mediterranean—when, I may say, he was acting in support of a villainous local dignitary whom His Majesty's Government did not in the least wish to see in a position of prominence—I could not, of course, contemplate with equanimity the prospect of his allying himself with your family, my dear Gwendolen! But the Marquis of Lyndale must certainly be a person of consequence, no matter what his past derelictions may be; and I cannot conceive of any prudent parent's not considering him a most eligible *parti*.

GWENDOLEN. Unfortunately, Jane is not a prudent parent, but a young girl—and a rather innocent, sensitive one, at that. I *do* think you ought to remember that, in answering my question.

BELVILLE (*tolerantly*) My dear Gwendolen, if the predilections and sensitivities of young ladies are to be the sole basis on which the serious matter of matrimony is decided, I am afraid we shall have a great many excessively imprudent marriages! One must, of course, be practical, above all.

GWENDOLEN (*rebelliously*) I don't believe Lord Nelson was practical. At least he may have been when he married, but afterwards, when Lady Hamilton came into the picture —

BELVILLE *(interrupting her, deeply shocked)* Miss Quarters! Gwendolen, that is! That is *not* a suitable subject —!

GWENDOLEN *(undeterred)* And what about yourself? *I* have no fortune, and yet you have offered for me —

BELVILLE (swallowing visibly, but speaking manfully) Yes.

GWENDOLEN (*regards him as if she rather expects something more. Nothing comes. BELVILLE's brows are knit; he is looking gloomy.*)

GWENDOLEN (*determinedly*) It *is* a very warm day — isn't it? Perhaps a bit too warm —

"And why," she said to herself, as she bit the end of her pen so hard that she left tooth-marks upon it, "I didn't tell him then and there that he was free as a bird as far as *I* was concerned, I *can't* think! Oh, Jupiter! *What* a muddle! Can *he* have changed so much, I wonder, or is it me?"

And Lyndale's words, "Of all the pompous, opinionated asses —!" came back to her like the pronouncement of some unusually unequivocal oracle, which should have warned her but unfortunately hadn't.

There was nothing for it now, of course, she told herself, but to release the Captain from their engagement as soon as possible. Obviously, he had found that tête-à-tête of theirs quite as unsatisfactory as she had—a somewhat lowering thought to one's *amour-propre*; but then it was far better, she thought, for them to have discovered at this stage that they would not suit than after the knot had been tied. The notion that her lack of fortune had had something to do with Belville's notable lack of enthusiasm over the prospect of marrying her did, of course, occur to her—"but still I don't think even *that* would have made him look so Friday-faced," she thought, "if I had only appeared to him the sort of milk-and-water female he seems to consider proper wife-material! Oh dear, why must men always want conformable wives? I had as well try to suit Lyndale as him!"

As to what her mama would say about this cavalier oversetting of one of her most cherished plans, she did not speculate, for she had no intention whatever of telling her of the disappointment in store for her until the matter had been settled with Belville and it was too late for anyone to do anything about it.

"I daresay," she said to herself, taking a resignedly philosophical point of view, "I am destined to be an aunt; but at any rate there is always plenty to do at Brightleaves, and I expect Papa and Mama would have missed me if I had actually married Henry—ugh!—and gone away and left them."

And such was the disillusionment wrought in her by the unfortunate impression the gallant Captain had made upon her that she wondered in an almost sacrilegious way whether Lord Nelson, too, had been a bit of a bore when not performing heroics upon the quarter-deck, and had set Lady Hamilton's back up with condescending speeches beginning, "My dear Emma," exactly as Belville had with her.

Six

"**I** have had," said Campaspe to Gwendolen the following morning, "the most *splendid* idea about how to rescue Jane!"

She sat perched upon the foot of Gwendolen's bed, having burst into her bedchamber to awaken her at an early hour of a wet morning. Gwendolen, opening one eye to take in the dim grey light and becoming conscious of a steady drumming of rain outside the window, burrowed into her pillow once more and muttered in an almost inaudible voice that Jane didn't need rescuing now.

"Yes, she does!" Campaspe insisted, leaning forward and poking the covers indiscriminately to make sure Gwendolen did not go to sleep again. "You didn't hear her last evening. She was going on about her *duty* again, and how she couldn't possibly go to Beauworth tomorrow, with the Duke and Lady Maria and everyone else thinking she was going to marry Lyndale, and then end by telling him she wouldn't. So I have decided to take matters into my own hands."

Gwendolen, with a decided feeling of foreboding, sat up and asked her what she meant to do.

"I intend," said Campaspe proudly, "to demonstrate to Mama — and to the world, in fact — that Lyndale is completely out of the question as a husband for Jane. Well, I mean to say, after all, a man who is engaged to one woman, and at the same time involves himself in an intrigue with another, *can't* be thought a suitable person to marry Jane — can he?"

Gwendolen, by this time perfectly wide awake, stared at her young sister in amazement.

"An intrigue with another?" she repeated blankly. "Lyndale? But who in the world — ?"

"Me," said Campaspe complacently.

"You!" Gwendolen smiled incredulously. "Oh, Cammie, don't be nonsensical!" she said. "*You* carrying on an intrigue with Lyndale! He would go into whoops at the very idea!"

"No, he wouldn't!" said Campaspe indignantly. "A great many older men *prefer* young girls; I am sure I have read that frequently!"

"Then you have been reading literature very unsuitable for your years," Gwendolen said firmly. "Really, Cammie, of all the birdwitted ideas — ! What would Neil have to say to it, do you think, if he saw you throwing yourself at Lyndale's head?"

Campaspe shrugged. "It might do him a great deal of good," she said with a very grown-up air. "Men are *so* much inclined to take one for granted!"

64

"Fiddle!" said Gwendolen. "Of course he takes you for granted; after all, he has known you since you were in short coats!" She got out of bed, wriggled her feet into her slippers, and stood facing her younger sister severely. "Cammie," she said, "I absolutely forbid you to give another thought to this skipbrained idea! In the first place, it would not serve—"

"Then *you* do it," Campaspe said inspirationally. "After all, *you* are far better acquainted with him than I am—"

"Not for worlds!" Gwendolen declared feelingly.

"Because of Captain Belville?"

"Because of my own self-respect! Lord Lyndale and I have already come to cuffs more than once. He knows exactly what I think of him, and, I daresay, when he learns I am not going to marry Belville, he would immediately consider, if I began casting out lures, that I was looking towards a greater fortune and a title—"

It was now Campaspe's turn to stare. "You're not going to marry Belville!" she repeated.

"No."

"Oh, Gwen, how perfectly, perfectly splendid!" Campaspe flew at her sister and kissed her enthusiastically. "I *didn't* like to say so yesterday, but he *is* a horrid man—so stiff and pompous! I can't think why you ever wanted to marry him!"

"Nor can I," Gwendolen confessed. "I expect it was because I didn't know him very well, and of course while he was away at sea I had no opportunity of finding out my mistake.

"Have you told him yet? Will he be very angry?"

"Very relieved, I should think," Gwendolen said coolly, "though I haven't had an opportunity to speak to him on the matter yet. I don't believe he wants to marry me any more than I want to marry him. And, after all, there is Evelina, with all that lovely Rutledge money, ready to drop into his lap like a ripe plum." She looked warningly at Campaspe. "But you mustn't tell any of this to Mama," she said. "I shall contrive to speak to Belville after dinner this evening, and *that* will be quite time enough for her to learn of it, when we have settled it all between us."

"Heavens! She *will* fly up into the boughs!" Campaspe said, looking awed but at the same time highly gratified at this prospect of approaching drama.

But, as matters fell out, neither was Belville to learn that evening of his miraculous escape from marriage with a portionless young lady, nor was Lady Otilia to suffer the mortification of seeing her cherished plan for marrying off her eldest daughter to an eligible suitor overset, for at four o'clock one of the Rutledge grooms arrived at Brightleaves, bearing a note from Mrs. Rutledge. Poor Henry, she wrote at greater length and with more obvious satisfaction than Lady Otilia considered decent, would unfortunately be unable to keep his engagement to dine with them that evening, having contracted a very nasty feverish cold, no doubt from sleeping between unaired sheets in that horrid inn where he had stopped in travelling up from Portsmouth. She could not recommend, she wrote, his exposing himself to the rain, but the Quarterses might rest assured that everything that could be done to make him comfortable and speed his recovery was being done for him under her roof, and that they might expect to see him at Brightleaves as soon as he was again himself.

Lady Otilia, being a gentlewoman, did not grind her

teeth or swear upon receiving this missive; but she made several highly uncharitable remarks about Mrs. Rutledge's motives in inducing Captain Belville to coddle himself to the extent of remaining by the fire with his feet in a steaming bath of mustard and water, eating thin gruel and slighting his social obligations, when there was no more amiss with him than a cold. She then declared her intention of calling at the Rutledges' the first thing in the morning, taking Gwendolen with her, for the purpose of ascertaining for herself how serious the Captain's indisposition actually was.

But to this plan Gwendolen entered an emphatic veto. Nothing, she declared, would induce her to intrude in Captain Belville's sick-room, engagement or no engagement, and she had almost come to the point of telling her mother that there would be no engagement as soon as she had managed to get a private word with her betrothed when fortunately Jane came into the room and Lady Otilia's maternal energies were diverted in the direction of endeavouring to discover whether she had decided to put off her missish temporising and accept Lord Lyndale's offer of marriage.

Lady Otilia's intention of calling at the Rutledges' received a further setback the following morning, when, before she could leave the house, a note was brought her from Captain Belville himself. In it he apologised once more for his inability to accept her invitation to dinner the previous evening and assured her that he was sufficiently improved to be able to look forward to meeting her and the young ladies at Beauworth that evening, Lady Maria having been kind enough to send him an invitation when she had learned he was staying in the neighbourhood.

"Well, I daresay we need not call in to see him this morning, after all, since we are assured of meeting him this evening," Lady Otilia said, though still with some lingering dissatisfaction in her manner. She read through the note once more. "He says nothing, I see, my dears," she observed, brightening, "of the Rutledges' having been invited as well, which is a decided snub to them, of course; but then the Duke simply will *not* have people at Beauworth who don't amuse him, no matter how odd it may sometimes seem. Poor Lady Maria was used to tell me — *before* the Duke and your papa had that unfortunate falling-out, naturally — how uncomfortable it often made her, but there is nothing that *she* can do."

It was Gwendolen's private opinion, which she communicated to Campaspe after Lady Otilia had left the room, that the Duke would find Captain Belville even less amusing than he would have found the Rutledges, but that no doubt, like herself, he knew him more by reputation than by nature and would soon discover his error. Jane, who was seated quietly in a corner of the room engaged in some of the exquisite needlework at which she excelled, and who had been almost forgotten by her sisters, looked up at this, with a slight, puzzled frown wrinkling her brows.

"But, Gwen," she protested mildly, "*you* don't think Captain Belville is dull — ?"

"Oh, don't she?" retorted Campaspe. "And, what's more, he *is* dull — only it doesn't matter now, because she's not going to marry him."

"Not going to —!" Jane let her needlework fall, her eyes growing round. "Oh, Gwen, you *aren't* going to jilt him!" she gasped.

"Well, yes, I expect I am," Gwendolen said judicially,

"if jilting means telling a man who obviously doesn't want to marry you that you don't want to marry him, either." She saw Jane's eyes fill with tears. "Now *don't* be a widgeon, Jane!" she said briskly. "It's *not* the tragic end of a beautiful love; after all, I haven't so much as clapped eyes on the man for two years, and it's quite, *quite* clear that I had my head in the clouds all that time and was imagining him to be a prince out of a fairy tale instead of the very ordinary man he is—"

Jane took out her handkerchief and determinedly wiped her eyes. "It's n-not that," she declared, her speech still slightly impeded by the emotion she was obviously endeavouring to repress. "If you don't w-wish to marry Captain Belville, of c-course you must not; only—only—*I* shall *have* to tell Lord Lyndale now that I will marry *him*—"

"Well, I don't see *that*!" Campaspe said roundly. "Why should *this* make a difference in what *you* do?"

Jane raised her brimming eyes to her face. "Mama," she said simply. "Oh, don't you see, Cammie?—we can't *both* disappoint her! It would be too cruel!"

Gwendolen and Campaspe looked at each other, appalled. It had never occurred to either of them that Jane would see the matter in this light, and after a moment's stunned silence they set themselves simultaneously to the task of convincing her that the mere fact that Gwendolen's engagement was to be broken off did not automatically require her to enter into one with Lyndale. Campaspe's arguments imaginatively included the prediction that Gwendolen, free now of her entanglement with Belville, would undoubtedly fascinate one—if not several—of the gentlemen of wealth and title whom the Duke always had staying at Beauworth, and

69

would be deluged with matrimonial prospects far more splendid than any Belville could offer, while Gwendolen threatened, if Jane did not promise to do nothing at present concerning Lyndale, to marry the odious Captain out of hand and be bored to death for the rest of her life.

"All the same," Campaspe said darkly when she and Gwendolen, having prevailed upon Jane to give them her word that she would take no immediate steps to enter into a definite engagement with Lyndale, went off together, "I don't trust her not to let her higher feelings get the better of her if she sees Mama falling into the dismals after you have sent Belville about his business. You may say what you like, Gwen, but something really *must* be done, and unless you can think of a better plan, *I* shall certainly go on with mine."

This declaration made Gwendolen even less happy when she contemplated the coming evening at Beau-worth, adding as it did a further complication to her own problem of being obliged to appear there as Belville's betrothed in company with the Captain himself. She had toyed with the idea of sending him a note in which she would politely but kindly inform him that their engagement was at an end, but had eventually decided that it would be far better to face the embarrassment of a public appearance as his betrothed than to break off with him in this cavalier fashion.

It required all the assurance given by her mirror, however, reflecting as it did the salutary effect made upon her appearance by the first really elegant evening-frock she had ever owned, to send her off to Beauworth that evening in a state of reasonable equanimity. Lady Otilia, regal in purple-bloom satin, had no such misgivings, and, indeed, any mother's heart might have swelled with satisfaction at sight of the three young ladies who foregathered with her in the shabby drawing room, ready to be conveyed to Beauworth in the lumbering old family coach. Jane, of course, was the undisputed beauty of the group, a fairy-tale princess in her gown of rose-pink gauze; but Gwendolen, in the almond-green gown, her fair hair dressed high on her head, with a few fascinating ringlets straying at nape and temples, was certainly in her best looks that evening; and even Campaspe, in a demure white muslin frock, her ruddy hair arranged à *l'Anglaise*, appeared very much the young lady of fashion.

All in all, Lady Otilia thought proudly, the Duke, who was well known to be a connoisseur of feminine beauty, would have every reason to regret the quarrel that had resulted in the exclusion of the Quarters family from the portals of Beauworth; and she confidently expected that, once he had set eyes on her daughters, this would be but the first of many occasions when they would appear within those august precincts. Of Mr. Quarters she quite despaired; he had refused to go to Beauworth that evening, saying that only the chance of having a long talk with Lyndale about his Arabian mares would have tempted him thither, and as Lyndale had come round that morning to look over his stables, and they had had a very satisfactory conversation then, there was really no need for him to put himself to that trouble.

So the Brightleaves ladies went off to Beauworth without him, and shortly afterwards their coach turned into the ducal grounds through the great gates and went clip-clopping up a winding lane, past an Embroidered Parterre, a Grotto, a Fountain, and an Arboretum of exotic trees, to the spectacular but quite hideous mansion, built in the fashionable Picturesque style, which the Duke, having taken a fancy some twenty years before to improve his Gloucestershire estate, had caused to be constructed upon the site of the more modest Jacobean house that had satisfied his ancestors. It resembled nothing so much as a mediaeval castle, with oriels and bays, a prodigious tower, and pepperpot-crowned corner turrets.

Inside, when the Quarters ladies entered, they found themselves in a staircase hall of seemingly vertiginous height, the stairs mounting in two flights to a first floor surrounded by marble arcades which were overshadowed by a corbelled gallery beneath a fan-vaulted coving.

"Jupiter!" Campaspe, who had never seen it before, whispered in Gwendolen's ear as they followed a stately butler up the long staircase. "Neil says he feels as if he ought to be wearing a suit of armour when he comes here, and I know now exactly what he means. Do you know he will be here tonight? The Fairhalls were asked, and the doctor said he might come."

"Sh-h-h!" said Gwendolen.

They were approaching the head of the staircase, where Lady Maria, without the Duke, but supported by a thin, fair, slight young man with delicate, distinguished-looking features, was standing to greet them.

"Alain!" hissed the irrepressible Campaspe, again in Gwendolen's ear. "I daresay Lady Maria needed him this evening to make up her table. Look at Jane! I do believe she is going to faint!"

Seven

Jane, however, had been far too well schooled during her London Season by Lady Priscilla to do anything so shockingly unfashionable as swooning away at sight of her beloved; and, though her lips quivered and her face was indubitably extremely pale, she managed a very creditable smile as she made her curtsey to Lady Maria and said good evening to M. de Combray—the latter, in truth, looking quite as white as she was herself. Fortunately, since the Fairhalls arrived just then and came up the stairs in something of a bustle, owing to the difficulty experienced by young Lieutenant Fairhall in managing the long flight with a leg that was still very lame from his wound, the two star-crossed young lovers had ample opportunity to regain control of their feelings before they entered the Long Gallery, where the Duke and his other guests had foregathered.

Lady Maria had spoken of a small party, but Gwendolen saw at a glance, as she entered this imposing apartment, with its hammer-beam roof and its windows filled with traceried lights in the Gothic style, that they would sit down at least twenty to dinner. In addition to the local guests and the members of the Duke's family, represented tonight by Lady Maria and the Duke's second son, Lord Wilfrid Boulting, she perceived at least half a dozen strangers whom she guessed to be staying at Beauworth, all attired in the latest London fashions and all apparently upon intimate terms with the Duke and with one another.

The Duke himself, a rather small man, looking a good deal older than his sixty-odd years, and with an air that managed to appear at the same time unceremonious and supercilious, was holding court from a large carved oak chair on the dais at the end of the long room, and thither Lady Otilia and her daughters were shepherded by an anxious Lady Maria.

"You remember Lady Otilia Quarters, I am sure, Papa — Miss Quarters — Miss Jane Quarters — Miss Campaspe —"

The Duke put up his quizzing-glass and stared at them, exactly, as Campaspe later indignantly said, like a judge at a cattle show.

"You will excuse my not rising, ma'am," he said to Lady Otilia perfunctorily, when he had quite completed his survey. "Touch of the gout." His grey eyes, still keen in his ravaged face, surveyed her sardonically. "Quarters doesn't appear — eh?" he barked. "Not surprised. Tell him I'll have that land of his yet." He beckoned to Jane. "Come here, my dear," he said, leering at her unbecomingly. "No need to ask which of you it is that Lyndale's fixed his choice on; you're the Beauty, and no mistake. Sit down here beside me. It ain't often I see such a pretty face."

This last comment, Gwendolen saw, did not appear at all to suit a tall, very handsome, dark-haired young woman, dressed in the height of fashion in an amber robe of satin and lace, who had been seated at his elbow, laughing and conversing with him, as the Quarterses had entered the room. She was presented to Lady Otilia by Lady Maria a few moments later as a Miss Courtney; and Captain Belville, who had come up to greet the party as soon as they had entered—waiting deferentially to pay his devoirs to them, however, until the Duke had dismissed them—impressively added the information in Gwendolen's ear that she was a great heiress, and connected on her mother's side not only with the family at Beauworth but also with many other of the most considerable families of England.

Gwendolen, seeing that, disappointed of the Duke, Miss Courtney had now turned her attention to Lyndale in a manner that scarcely seemed to take into account the well-known reason for his being in Gloucestershire, said critically that she was very handsome, but she, Gwendolen, hardly thought she would suit Lord Lyndale.

"Suit Lord Lyndale! Indeed, I should think she would not," said Captain Belville, looking shocked, "since he has already offered for your sister!"

"Well, there's many a slip 'twixt cup and lip, you know," Gwendolen said philosophically, wishing she might tell the Captain then and there that there was going to be a very large slip 'twixt the cup and the lip of *their* marriage. "But even if he doesn't marry Jane in the end," she went on, "I *do* think Miss Courtney is wasting her time. She doesn't appear to me to be in the least the sort of young woman Lord Lyndale wishes for a wife."

Probably to Captain Belville's relief—for he was looking very much nonplussed at his beloved's cool assessment of Lyndale's matrimonial preferences—their conversation was interrupted at this point by Alain de Combray, who came up, in his rather hesitating, diffident way, to express his pleasure to Gwendolen at seeing her again, after a considerable length of time during which they had not met. He had always been a favourite of hers, ever since he had first come to Beauworth a little over a year before as the latest in the succession of secretaries to the irascible Duke. She found him pleasant and intelligent, with agreeable manners and quiet tastes, and had long felt that, except for the problem of fortune, he and Jane might have been made for each other.

She saw a shadow now in his face, however, that had not used to be there, noticed how often his eyes strayed to where Jane sat in blushing conversation with the Duke, and wished she might have been able to give him some comfort in regard to his future. But the only comfort she could reasonably offer was the information that Campaspe had decided Jane was not to marry Lyndale, which seemed to her rather a broken reed for anyone to rely upon.

She did observe, however, with some misgiving, that Campaspe had already begun her campaign to cause Lyndale to appear a heartless libertine, bent upon toying with the affections of one sister while making honourable offers of marriage to another, for she had now managed, by a boldness of manoeuvre that would have shocked Lady Otilia had she been able to withdraw her eyes from the pleasing spectacle of the Duke admiring Jane's beauty, to detach Lyndale from Miss Courtney and was engaging him in animated conversation.

Fortunately, the announcement of dinner put an end to this improper tête-à-tête (or at least it was as improper as Campaspe knew how to make it), and the company all went down to the great dining room, which was extremely large and mediaeval and would no doubt have had rushes strewn on the floor and minstrels playing on sackbuts and hautboys if the Duke had not detested music and preferred Aubusson carpets to floor coverings taken directly from nature. Gwendolen found herself seated between Captain Belville and Lord Wilfrid Boulting, and was relieved to see that Campaspe had been placed quite at the other end of the table from Lyndale, who had Jane on one side and Miss Courtney on the other. Regarding Miss Courtney with some disfavour —for that enterprising young lady had not wasted a moment, once she found herself seated beside the Marquis, in claiming his attention, quite regardless of good manners—Gwendolen thought that if Campaspe wished for a likely female to enter into an intrigue with Lyndale, the dashing Miss Courtney was certainly proclaiming herself to be available.

A voice at her elbow broke in upon these reflections.

"I know," said Lord Wilfrid Boulting, in the faintly supercilious drawl that even the famous Mr. Brummell himself could not have improved upon for sheer sweetly self-centred arrogance, "that by all the canons of social usage you should be conversing with Belville, Miss Quarters, but since Frieda Courtney is upsetting the whole table by talking to Lyndale, may I join in the general anarchy by holding converse with you? Besides, you can't really wish to talk to Belville. I don't know why it is that naval men are always either tediously jolly or overwhelmingly dull, but so it is. The gallant Captain, I should say from brief observation, falls into the latter category."

Gwendolen stared at him, not quite certain whether to be affronted or amused. She had never met Lord Wilfrid before, as he spent very little time at Beauworth and at any rate would have had no time at all for the rather untidy schoolgirl she had been before the celebrated quarrel between the Duke and Mr. Quarters had broken off intercourse between the two families, and she wondered now if she thought him handsome. Probably not, she decided, since his eyes were too close together, his features undistinguished, and his figure somewhat thickset; but as an indisputable member of the exclusive Bow-window Set he appeared to know how to make an air of absolute self-confidence take the place of mere physical endowments.

"You can't," she remarked to him, once she had decided this point, "be aware, I think, sir, that Captain Belville and I are betrothed. But, pray," she added kindly, "don't let it embarrass you."

"On the contrary," said Lord Wilfrid, "I am quite aware of it, and I am not at all embarrassed. I find it so much easier, you see, to get on with people if I am perfectly frank with them, regardless of the proprieties. All of which leads me to remark that I cannot think why a perfectly charming girl like you should wish to be married to a naval man, which appears to me in all respects a fate worse than death, involving as it does widowhood — practically speaking — for a goodly portion of one's life, without the consolation of being able to cast one's eyes about for a suitable replacement."

Gwendolen, looking at him with some interest, said it was remarkable, but she hadn't thought of that.

"I daresay," she said thoughtfully, "it is because I never got that far. I mean, when you are engaged it seems somehow a quite permanent state of affairs, or at least one never actually gets beyond the wedding in one's mind. After that, it's like having to imagine what happens to the characters after you've read the last chapter of a novel. That is, if they aren't dead, as they mostly seem to be in tragedies."

"But you and the Captain," pursued Lord Wilfrid, evidently intrigued out of his customary boredom by her matter-of-fact reply to his rather provocative speech, "will not be dead, presumably, Miss Quarters."

"Oh, no," said Gwendolen. "But, on the other hand, we won't be —"

She caught herself up. She had been about to say, "We won't be married, either," but it had occurred to her just in time that it would be not only improper but also highly unwise to let Lord Wilfrid (who looked as if he would be good at remembering secrets and making use of them for his own advantage) learn, before she had informed the Captain himself of the fact, that she had no present intention of marrying Belville.

Lord Wilfrid, as she had feared he would, at once took up her suspended words.

'You won't be what?" he enquired.

"Oh — nothing," Gwendolen said vaguely. "I forget what I was saying. This is a splendid room, isn't it? But rather overpowering. You don't come to Beauworth often, do you?"

Lord Wilfrid's thin, sandy brows went up. "So many red herrings!" he said. "I suspect there must be something behind them all. You and the Captain won't be—what, Miss Quarters? Could the missing word possibly be—married?"

"Well, of course we would be married if we *got* married," Gwendolen said, confusing the issue with a false air of frankness. "Only people sometimes don't—do they? Take Jane and Lord Lyndale, for example—"

"I should like very much to take Jane," said Lord Wilfrid, extremely improperly. "As for Lyndale, he is exactly the sort of man one does so wish would never appear to blight the social scene. He has *no* tact, says exactly what he thinks to my ducal papa, so that life becomes a matter of nerve-shattering explosions when they are together, and exhibits a shocking lack of reverence for his Boulting blood. And *so* like him (if you will forgive my saying it, but of course you will; I have never met a young lady who seemed so totally tolerant) to fix his choice on a little provincial nobody, when he might have his choice of the current crop of London Beauties. Look at Miss Courtney, for example. *She* won't give up the hunt until the happy couple walks out the door of St. George's, Hanover Square."

"Well, I think it would be charitable of you to tell her, then, that she is wasting her time," Gwendolen said decidedly. "Lord Lyndale wants a conformable wife; he has told me so himself. And Jane is nothing if not conformable. I do wish she weren't!"

Lord Wilfrid's sandy brows once more ascended. "Am I to understand," he enquired, "that you don't wish your sister to marry Lyndale? How very odd!" Gwendolen said nothing. "*Don't* you?" he persisted.

"Well—not if they won't be happy together," Gwendolen said, rather ambiguously.

Lord Wilfrid smiled. It was not his custom to laugh, or he looked as if he would have done so. "My dear good child," he said with an air of tolerant condescension, "you really must not talk like the heroine of a sentimental novel. It is *quite* out of fashion in London circles to consider that marriage must have any connexion with love."

"Yes, but, you see, I have never been to London."

"You should go. You *must* go. I shall sponsor your entrance myself into the most exclusive circles, and you will be the rage of the town. But *not*," he warned, "if you make sentimental speeches, and *not* if you are married to the naval hero at your elbow. Are you *quite* sure that you *must* take that fatal step?"

"Well—one never knows, does one?" Gwendolen said judicially. "You see, I rather think *he* wants a conformable wife, too, and I am not at all conformable." She looked at Lord Wilfrid speculatively. "Would you really take me up if I went to London?" she demanded. "I daresay you are a person of extreme importance there? You look as if you are, and, after all, you *are* a duke's son."

"Being a duke's son," said Lord Wilfrid with hauteur, "has nothing to do with it, my dear Miss Quarters. I *am* an extremely important person in London, but it is genius that has raised me to the eminence I occupy. The arrangement of my neckcloth, the cut of my coat, the exquisite manner in which I take snuff—these are all points upon which I admittedly excel, subjects which I have studied to a degree of mastery that is the despair of those who would emulate me— Am I boring you?" he broke off to demand with some acerbity, as he saw that Gwendolen's attention was obviously wandering from his words.

"Well, yes, you are, rather," Gwendolen said, smiling at him agreeably. "How very acute of you to realise it! Most people don't, you know. They *will* go prosing on forever about something that is not of the least interest to one. But I daresay it is your wide experience in Society that has made you more perceptive about such things than most people are." As Lord Wilfrid, who had never, in the dozen years since he had come upon the town, been informed that he was anything less than a *premier* conversationalist, merely gazed at her, for once stunned into silence, she went on amicably, "At any rate, I really must talk to Belville now; he is looking quite sulky over our behaving so badly. But, remember, if ever I *do* get up to London, I shall expect your patronage."

She thereupon turned her attention to Captain Belville, who was, indeed, looking very much put out by her neglect of her social duties. It was not an easy matter to induce him to enter into civil conversation with her, and when he did, she was even more bored than she had been by Lord Wilfrid's praise of his own "genius," for his one topic appeared to be a reverential inventory of the splendours of Beauworth. Prodded out of that, he fell into praise of the dinner that was being set before them, with a few *sotto voce* remarks (interspersed amid his encomiums on the sauté of fillets of fowl à la Lucullus and the fricandeau de veau), concerning the exalted rank of their fellow guests, upon which he appeared to have made minute enquiries of Lady Maria.

All in all, Gwendolen was heartily glad when Lady Maria took her ladies away to the great Crimson Saloon, leaving the gentlemen to enjoy their wine in the dining room.

But she soon found that social life among the female

contingent at Beauworth was even more unrewarding than it had been in mixed company, for she was not only bored, she was also snubbed, particularly by the dashing Miss Courtney, who made amused comments behind her fan to her friends about "provincial Beauties," laughed a great deal over witticisms with references that were entirely lost on the ladies from Brightleaves, and perseveringly looked right through Gwendolen out of large, condescending, oxlike eyes (the last uncomplimentary adjective was Gwendolen's) whenever the latter ventured to speak.

Lady Maria, quite obviously wretched over the bad manners of her London guests, was yet too timid to take the conversation in hand herself, and so matters stood until the arrival of the gentlemen broke off the uncomfortable situation.

Eight

The Duke, who, though his own dancing days were over, much enjoyed watching a bevy of attractive young ladies engaged in waltzes and country dances, had arranged for an orchestra to play after dinner, and for one of Beauworth's large saloons to be cleared for dancing, the ballroom, as he remarked to Lady Otilia, being far too large for a mere six or eight couples.

Gwendolen expected that she would be obliged to stand up with Belville for the first set, and was looking forward to this without a great deal of enthusiasm, for she had already had her fill of hearing him go into raptures over the glories of Beauworth, and remembered, besides, that as a dancer he was more dogged than expert, when she suddenly found herself being approached by Lyndale, who came strolling up to her with the same lack of ceremony he had displayed upon their previous meetings and asked her to partner him in the set of country dances that was forming.

"But shouldn't you ask Jane?" Gwendolen enquired, looking at him rather dubiously, for in spite of the fact that she had no desire for him to press his suit upon her sister, neither did she wish to see Jane slighted.

"Not at all," said Lyndale promptly. "That is Wilfrid's honour, as the Duke's representative. He has already claimed her hand."

"Oh—very well, then," Gwendolen agreed. "I daresay it will be better than standing up with Belville, at any rate, and I am sure he has the intention of asking me. I am very sorry, Henry," she went on as the Captain, just on cue, appeared at her elbow and opened his mouth to speak, "but Lord Lyndale has already asked me to stand up with him for this set. Why don't you go and dance with Cammie? Lieutenant Fairhall, as you can see, can scarcely hobble, much less dance, and these London people seem so taken up with each other that I am afraid none of them will think of asking her."

The unhappy Belville, finding himself again Slighted for Another, as Gwendolen had no doubt he was expressing it in his own mind, compressed his lips and looked at Lyndale in a highly unfriendly fashion; but then, apparently recollecting that rank had its privileges, bowed to him somewhat stiffly, said he, Lyndale, was indeed happy in his choice, and walked away.

"You *aren't* going to marry that fellow, are you?" Lyndale asked in tones of some amusement, as he led Gwendolen into the set. "I seem to detect a distinct lack of loverlike ardour in your behaviour towards him this evening. Being a gentleman, I shan't hint, of course, that he scarcely appears overcome, either, by your fatal beauty and his own passionate feelings."

"But you *have* hinted it," Gwendolen pointed out. "In fact, you have said it very plainly." She looked critically across the room at the Captain's tall, high-shouldered figure bowing over Campaspe's hand. "And perhaps it *is* true," she acknowledged, "that he is not overcome by his feelings, but, on the other hand, you must admit that he is very obedient, which is an excessively desirable quality in a husband. I am sure he will make an excellent one."

"But *not*," Lyndale said positively, "for you."

"Oh? Why not?" she asked innocently. She might not have the least intention, she said to herself, of marrying Belville, but she was certainly not going to give the Marquis the satisfaction of hearing from her lips how correct he had been in his estimate of the Captain's character.

Lyndale, however, merely said in a maddeningly matter-of-fact way that if she didn't already know that, she would find out soon enough after she had married him, and then turned the subject to Campaspe, enquiring what the devil the chit was about this evening.

"If I weren't an extremely modest sort of fellow, I might imagine she was throwing herself at my head," he said. "I thought she was engaged to young Fairhall."

"Sh-h-h!" said Gwendolen reprovingly, casting a meaningful glance at the other dancers.

"Nonsense!" said Lyndale. "They are all flirting with one another so madly that they wouldn't notice if we suddenly began doing a Highland reel or singing "God Save the King". I never saw such an amount of ogling and sighing as goes on in polite circles in England; there would be throats cut and daggers flashing all over the place if half as much of it took place in Morocco. Fortunately, the female sex is given far less scope there to practise its wiles."

"I daresay you mean harems," Gwendolen said, strongly disapproving, but unable to resist the promptings of curiosity. "*Do* tell me about them! Do the women wear trousers and—?"

"My dear Miss Quarters!" interrupted Lyndale, with a slight, significant lift of the brows and a glance at the other dancers. "Pray consider *my* reputation, if not your own!"

"But you said they were paying no heed— Oh, you are joking me!" Gwendolen broke off to say severely. "What an abominable man you are!"

"Because I won't talk to you about harems? That is mere self-preservation. If I were to do so, you would no doubt treat me to a bear-jaw on the inhumanity of the male sex."

"Well, I *don't* think it must be a very invigorating life," Gwendolen said decidedly, "being shut up like that and having no one to talk to but a lot of other wives. *I* should think one would turn into a dead bore eventually, which, it seems to me, wouldn't be very agreeable for the husband, either."

Lyndale assured her, with an air of gravity that she regarded with some suspicion, that he did not believe she would turn into a dead bore even in a harem, which he fancied would be considerably enlivened by her presence, adding that, in his experience, gentlemen in Morocco unfortunately did not place a great deal of emphasis upon the conversational abilities of their wives. He then forestalled any adverse comment upon this state of affairs by bringing up the matter of Campaspe and demanding once more to know what she was about.

"I don't know," said Gwendolen, who would have died rather than betray her young sister, no matter how strongly she disapproved of her plan. She looked vaguely at the wall before her, where a stupendous rose-coloured tapestry, woven at Beauvais, displayed a number of buxom nymphs floating on pink clouds around a self-satisfied Jove, and went on, under inspiration, "Perhaps she has fallen in love with you."

"A likely story," said Lyndale, grinning.

"Oh?" Gwendolen raised her black, flyaway brows at him. "Don't women usually? I should have thought quite a few of them must have."

He nodded coolly. "Oh, quite a few," he said outrageously. "Which is why I know the signs, Miss Quarters. And I may tell you that your young sister displays none of them."

"Does Miss Courtney?" enquired Gwendolen, with an air of great innocence. "*She* seems very much interested in you."

Lyndale cast a glance across the room at Miss Courtney, who, having rejected several applications for the honour of standing up with her in favour of sitting beside the Duke, was allowing him to hold her hand under her fan.

"Miss Courtney," he said dryly, "is very much interested in my title and my fortune, but I doubt that there is any love for me stirring in her maiden heart. Now *don't* tell me," he went on, as Gwendolen opened her mouth to speak, "that Miss Campaspe has also decided that a marchioness's robes would suit her better than they would your sister Jane, Miss Quarters, because I will tell *you*, *that* cock won't fight."

"Oh, no!" said Gwendolen seriously. "Cammie cares nothing for title and fortune; I shouldn't dream of trying to tell you such a rapper. By the bye, I haven't thanked you yet for taking my advice about Jane. I consider that you behaved very nicely in that matter."

"Do you, indeed?" said Lyndale, politely but very non-committally, and as they were separated at that moment by the movement of the dance, she had no opportunity to continue on the subject.

When they were able to resume their conversation, Lyndale seemed more interested in discussing horses than people, having the highest opinion, he said, of the chances of Mr. Quarters's Conqueror in the Cheltenham Races, and as Gwendolen, though by no means so horse-mad as her father, had a good deal of knowledge about the equine species and was an excellent horsewoman and whip herself, the conversation went on in such an interesting fashion that before she knew it the set was at an end.

The last strains of music had only just died away when she found Campaspe and Captain Belville beside her.

"Oh, Lord Lyndale," Campaspe said, addressing the Marquis in what Gwendolen, with great vexation, saw she obviously considered the air of a dashing woman of the world, "I do hope you are going to ask me to stand up with you for this next set! I am dying to ask you all about Morocco — or is it Algeria? — and the native dances, which I am sure you must have learned to perform to perfection!"

Lyndale cocked an eyebrow at Gwendolen in a way

that caused her to think seriously of murdering him. "That is very kind of you," he said to Campaspe, "but don't you think I ought to ask your sister Jane to stand up with me before I ask you? As a matter of fact, Miss Quarters has just been reminding me of my duty in that respect."

"Oh," said Campaspe, quite undaunted, "Jane isn't in the least accustomed to standing upon her dignity! And," with a coaxing air, "I do *so* want to hear all about Algeria!"

Gwendolen saw that Captain Belville was looking quite aghast at this unblushing exhibition of the pursuing female, and that Lieutenant Fairhall, who was seated near enough to their little group to hear what was being said, had an expression of thunderstruck disapproval upon his fresh, youthful face. Deciding on the instant to take matters into her own hands, she said curtly, "*Don't* be a ninnyhammer, Cammie! Of course Lord Lyndale wishes to dance with Jane! Come along; I'll take you to Mama."

And she swept her unwilling young sister relentlessly off, quite undisturbed by the word, "Traitress!" hissed into her ear by Campaspe.

"*Have* you seen Alain?" Campaspe went on fiercely, as they approached the sofa from which Lady Otilia was complacently observing the dancing. "He looks *quite* ill! Have you *no* sense of human compassion?"

"I shall have none for you, if you don't put an end to this ridiculous pursuit of Lyndale at once!" Gwendolen promised her forcefully. "Now *do* sit down beside Mama and try for some conduct!"

Campaspe, looking mulish, suffered herself with the greatest unwillingness to be installed upon the sofa beside

Lady Otilia. Gwendolen, turning to face what she considered would be the inevitable application from Captain Belville, who had followed them across the room, to stand up with him for the next set, found herself adroitly intercepted at the same moment by Lord Wilfrid.

"Miss Quarters—will you do me the honour—?" he said, bowing slightly and offering her his arm.

Gwendolen looked at the Captain, but he, with a face that clearly displayed the conflict going on in the inner man between the jealousy of the betrothed lover and reverence for a title, merely compressed his lips, looked black, and said nothing.

"Oh, very well!" Gwendolen said to Lord Wilfrid, and walked off with him to join the set.

Lord Wilfrid at once began to talk about an impromptu picnic that he was planning for the following day.

"It came to me as I was dancing with the lovely Jane," he said, "that I must see the three sisters, like the Three Graces, strolling arm in arm upon the greensward in a leafy glade. I can never remember their names—the Three Graces, that is—though I am quite sure none of them was called Jane; but Gwendolen and Campaspe would seem suitable, even if not entirely accurate."

Gwendolen said she thought one of them was called Euphrosyne, which was even worse than Campaspe, and that she believed Jane would have been called that if they had not fortunately happened to have a great-aunt named Jane who had a little money.

"And I should dearly love to go on a pic-nic," she said. "We all should. Are we to drive or ride? And where are we to go?"

Lord Wilfrid, looking at her askance, said she could

not possibly wish to go jauntering about the countryside in such sultry weather as they were having at present.

"Well, but how are we to have a pic-nic, then?" Gwendolen demanded practically.

"We shall," Lord Wilfrid said, shrugging languidly, "have it here, on the grounds of Beauworth, of course, Miss Quarters. I seldom stray beyond the gates when I make one of my rare excursions into Gloucestershire. I find the country so excessively vulgar, you see — all that fresh air, and then I believe there are cows — "

"Oh, yes, quite a few of them," Gwendolen assured him. "I rather like them — but then I have never been to London."

"We are going to remedy that, if you will remember. Are you still engaged to the prosaic Captain?"

"Yes, of course; how could I have become *un*engaged at a dinner party, even if I wished to? But perhaps I shan't be some day. One never knows," said Gwendolen, regarding Lord Wilfrid thoughtfully.

She knew enough of the fashionable world, from reading and from having come into occasional improving contact with such persons as her aunt, Lady Priscilla, to be aware that Lord Wilfrid had none of the earmarks of a marrying man; and she wondered with a good deal of anticipation if she might eventually receive an improper proposal from him. On the whole she thought him, in his own way, almost as boring as the Captain; but one could not pick and choose when it came to improper proposals, and the romantic part of her nature that she had inherited from Lady Otilia at once began formulating a dramatic scene in which Lord Wilfrid, finding himself spurned by a virtuous female, gave vent to the lower side of his nature in an attempt to force her compliance to his will, only to be thwarted by the arrival of her gallant betrothed, Captain Belville, who would worst him decisively in single combat.

The one flaw in this picture was that she could not envision any circumstance under which Captain Belville would so far forget the deference due a member of the higher nobility as to attack Lord Wilfrid; but then, she thought hopefully, he might turn out to have hidden depths. After all, as she had so justly observed to Lord Wilfrid, one never knew.

Lord Wilfrid's attentions to Gwendolen, at any rate, were very satisfactorily assiduous during the remainder of the set—so much so, in fact, that when it had ended and Captain Belville was at last successful in obtaining her hand for the next set, he was in the sulks to such an extent that he scarcely vouchsafed a word of conversation to her all the while they were dancing. She saw Lyndale, who had asked—to Miss Courtney's obvious displeasure—one of the other ladies of the London party to stand up with him, regarding them with the air of detached amusement that appeared to Gwendolen to constitute his usual response to her discomfitures, and, gritting her teeth, began determinedly chattering away to the unresponsive Belville.

At last the set came to an end, and she was free to leave the Captain to his sullens and go and sit beside young Lieutenant Fairhall, who also appeared to be finding the evening a far from satisfactory one. In the first place, he cared nothing for the ducal splendours of Beauworth; in the second place, he could not dance; and in the third place, he was obviously seething with frustration and jealousy over the fact that Campaspe had paid not the least attention to him all evening, but instead was making what he characterised as a dashed cake of herself running after Lyndale.

"What the deuce does she think she is up to?" he demanded wrathfully. "Lord! if ever I saw such a cork-brained wag-feather! Lyndale has offered for Jane, hasn't he? They're as good as engaged, my mother says—and Cammie and I *are* engaged, dash it all! It's my belief she must be queer in her attic this evening!"

Gwendolen did her best to soothe him, but was somewhat perplexed as to how to convince him that Campaspe was impelled by the purest of motives in her pursuit of Lyndale without actually confiding that motive to him. And that, she was certain, would not do at all. She was very fond of Neil, but he had not much more discretion, she thought, than Campaspe, and if she were to tell him that Campaspe was doing her best to see to it that Jane was not obliged to marry Lyndale because she was in love with Alain de Combray, the matter would soon be spread over the entire neighbourhood.

So she told him instead that he must realize that Campaspe was very young, and that she, Gwendolen, would Speak to Her—which, indeed, she did, but without the slightest effect, for Campaspe, flown with the excitement of what she called the first really grown-up party she had ever attended, was in no mood to accept prudent counsel. She declared instead that she was going to ask Lyndale again to stand up with her, and, crossing the room to the place where he stood, proceeded at once to do so. Gwendolen, following her, was soon involved in a somewhat heated but outwardly amiable (for the sake of Miss Courtney, who was standing nearby) conversation with her, which was suddenly brought to an end, as the orchestra began to play, by Lyndale's leading her, not Campaspe, on to the floor.

"Oh, dear! Ought I? Shouldn't you rather have asked Miss Courtney?" she asked a trifle distractedly, feeling a bit like a Sabine maiden being swept off by a ruthless Roman, for the orchestra was playing a waltz and instead of facing her partner decorously across a safe distance of parquet floor she was in his arms, being whirled down the room in his masterful embrace. "After all, this is the second time this evening, and you have not danced once with her —"

"Miss Quarters," said Lyndale, "if you do not stop telling me whom I ought and ought not to dance with, I shall do something drastic —"

"But what *could* you do?" Gwendolen interrupted, much interested. "You could *not* listen to me, of course, but that isn't *drastic* —"

"Well, for one thing, I could dance with *you* for the rest of the evening," Lyndale said.

"No, you couldn't, for I shouldn't stand up with you," Gwendolen said promptly. "You don't waltz particularly well, you know; you are far too intent upon going your own way, so that even if it were proper for me to stand up so often with you, I don't think I should enjoy it. But I expect they don't do the waltz in Morocco, so you have not had an opportunity to learn it properly. I admit I am not very expert at it myself, for it is not danced much here in the country, but Jane has been trying to teach me since she returned from London. *She* performs it beautifully."

"So I see," said Lyndale, looking quite unperturbed by her strictures upon his terpsichorean abilities.

His eyes went across the room to where Jane, who had

95

allowed Alain de Combray to lead her on to the floor, was gliding with him in long, dreamy circles down the room. Her lips were slightly parted; her cheeks were suffused with soft, glowing colour; and Gwendolen saw with some dismay that her blue eyes, fixed upon the young Frenchman's face, were shining with a kind of mournful intensity that could not fail to strike anyone observing her. She stole a quick glance at Lyndale's face. It appeared quite calm, but rather thoughtful.

"They make," he remarked presently, "a handsome pair — your sister and young M. de Combray, Miss Quarters."

"Yes, indeed!" agreed Gwendolen, trying to conceal an uncomfortable feeling over the turn the conversation was taking and speaking, she immediately felt, rather too enthusiastically. She then tried to remedy matters by saying in a disparaging tone that almost any gentleman appeared to advantage when dancing with Jane.

"As I have told you, she learned to waltz beautifully in London," she said.

"And learned a great many other things there, as well, I expect," said Lyndale, still in that thoughtful voice. He looked down at Gwendolen abruptly. "Will you and your sisters attend Wilfrid's pic-nic tomorrow?" he asked, changing the subject abruptly.

Gwendolen, slightly surprised, said she expected they would if Lady Otilia found no objection to it, and she saw no reason why she should.

"Why do you ask?" she demanded.

"Mere curiosity," said Lyndale briefly, which she had no difficulty in interpreting as a polite euphemism for, "That is none of your affair, Miss Quarters."

She looked at him suspiciously. She had the feeling

that he had some plan in mind, a plan that in some way involved Jane and Alain de Combray, and she found it necessary to suppress a sigh of exasperation over the tangled state of affairs that made it expedient for her to be alarmed at this notion. If only Jane would make up her mind, she thought, to tell Lyndale that she did not wish to marry him, and to throw in her fortunes with Alain, even though they were to be as poor as church-mice and Brightleaves fell into the hands of Messrs. Smith and Brown, one would know where one stood and could act accordingly.

As it was, she did not know whether to be glad or sorry that Lyndale had seen that look upon Jane's face; but on the whole she felt a bit nervous about it. Gentlemen who had spent an extended period of time in Morocco might, she felt, have taken some rather peculiar ideas about af-fianced wives (even if they weren't *officially* affianced) who looked at other gentlemen in the particularly significant way Jane had looked at M. de Combray; and even if they hadn't, she had the feeling that Lyndale was unpredictable, at best.

However, there was nothing she could do about it but to warn Jane, after they had returned to Brightleaves that night, against looking at Alain at all if she wasn't able to manage her eyes better when she did; but as they were all rather tired by the time they did return, and Jane seemed already in the lowest of spirits, she eventually decided not to broach the subject.

Nine

On the following day a splendid barouche upholstered in plum-coloured velvet and with a ducal crest on the panel arrived at Brightleaves to take the three young ladies to Beauworth, Lady Otilia having declined an invitation to accompany them for the ostensible reason that it was the day upon which she customarily visited the sick and needy in the village, but actually because she had an obscure feeling that Lyndale might take the occasion to bring Jane to the point if no prospective mother-in-law were in the picture. She had satisfied herself, of course, that Lady Maria and one of the London ladies, a Mrs. Webley, would be present as chaperons, and thus felt no need to worry her head over the proprieties.

Gwendolen, wearing a fawn-coloured gown and a broad-brimmed Villager hat tied under her chin with brown velvet ribbons, both sent from London by Lady

Priscilla, was in her best looks, which gave her the courage, as she stepped into the carriage, to face the private interview she was determined to have that afternoon with Captain Belville with more equanimity than she could otherwise have done. As for Jane, she looked more beautiful than ever in an azure-blue gown and bonnet that matched her eyes, while Campaspe had done her best to offset the very youthful appearance conferred upon her by her sprig muslin frock by running downstairs at the last minute in one of Lady Otilia's turbans and a pair of long pebble earrings, well aware that there would not be time for the exhausting battle her mother and sisters knew they would be obliged to go through before she could be induced to return to her bedchamber and put on some more suitable headgear.

As a result, she rode off in triumph in the barouche, still wearing the turban, which elicited a considerable number of stares and some tittering behind fans from the ducal guests when she arrived at Beauworth—all of which she accepted with great aplomb, considering the attention she was receiving a tribute to her fashionable appearance. To Gwendolen's intense displeasure, she at once attached herself to Lyndale, which she had received the strictest of instructions not to do, and hung perseveringly upon his arm as the party strolled out of the house into the gardens.

"*Don't* encourage her!" Gwendolen, escaping from Belville, who had come up to offer her *his* arm with the air of a man eating green fruit but determined to look as if he was enjoying it, hissed emphatically into the Marquis's ear.

Lyndale looked round at her. "Oh, she doesn't need encouragement," he assured her. "No more than a limpet does. You might ask her, though, not to lean quite so heavily. Otherwise I am afraid I may be pretty well exhausted before the day has more than begun."

Gwendolen, her cheeks scarlet with embarrassment, said fiercely to Campaspe, "If you have no consideration for your own reputation, you *might* have some for your family! Don't you see Lord Lyndale doesn't *wish* for your company? Go and walk with Neil!"

Campaspe made a face at her. "I can't, she said. "Neil is angry with me. Besides, Lyndale and I were going on splendidly together before you came to interfere. Weren't we, my lord?" she asked, looking up at him with what she obviously considered a dashingly flirtatious expression upon her face.

"Well, at least we were keeping each other out of mischief," Lyndale conceded. "But why don't you join us yourself, Miss Quarters? With one of you on each arm, I don't think even Miss Campaspe will expect me to go beyond the line."

"*Two* ladies all to yourself, Lyndale! Unfair—palpably unfair!" said Lord Wilfrid, coming up at the same moment with his usual expression of rather disagreeably condescending good humour upon his face. "Miss Quarters, I claim your company as indisputably my due. Will you allow me to show you the gardens before the heat becomes quite too insupportable for strolling about? My papa has spared no expense on them, so naturally they must be admired."

Gwendolen, unable to think of a proper way of suggesting Campaspe as a substitute to Lord Wilfrid, or, indeed, of any way at all of inducing Campaspe to leave Lyndale, said in despair that she would be delighted. Of course she knew that in leaving Belville, first to talk to

Lyndale and then to walk off with Lord Wilfrid, she was presenting him with reason to turn quite as sulky as he had been on the previous evening; but at any rate, she thought, she was determined to give him his *congé* that day as soon as she was able to lure him away to a sufficiently secluded spot, and instinct told her that it might be easier to dismiss a lover who was already quite cross with one than one who was in an excellent temper.

What really concerned her was leaving Campaspe with Lyndale, to go as far in her hoydenish misbehaviour as his lordship, who seemed to have no sense of propriety whatever, would allow; and here she felt she must place all her dependance upon Miss Courtney, who had obviously not abandoned the pursuit and could probably be counted upon to appear upon the scene before long and turn that particular tête-à-tête into a conversation *à trois*.

So she went off with Lord Wilfrid with no more than a parting glance at Campaspe, meant to convey to her the awful consequences that would befall her if she did not conduct herself properly, but unfortunately quite ignored by her young sister and intercepted with appreciative amusement by Lyndale.

But both Campaspe and his lordship were soon to fly right out of Gwendolen's mind; for she and Lord Wilfrid had scarcely progressed from the "English" garden, laid out in eighteenth-century fashion with rose beds, flower borders, and statues of shepherds and shepherdesses, to the more elaborate Italian garden, when she discovered that Lord Wilfrid, like Campaspe, had no intention of allowing the grass to grow under his feet that day. As he invited her to pause on the stone-balustraded terrace overlooking the water-lily pool that was the centrepiece of this formal garden, and to admire its bronze fountain and the lavishly planted parterres that surrounded it, she found an arm slipped insinuatingly about her waist. When she moved carelessly away, pretending to ignore the arm and feigning an interest in a wild garden just visible to one side in the valley below, she was led into a yew walk which too late she saw secluded them entirely from the possibility of being observed by anyone who had not, like themselves, entered that long, green, narrow alley.

"Ravishing creature!" said Lord Wilfrid, who, had she known it, preferred to carry on his amours in a rather eighteenth-century style, and lost his r's almost entirely when involved in them, so that "ravishing creature!" came out more like "wavishing cweature!" "When am I to be rewarded, my charming angel," he went on, passing that insinuating arm once more about her waist, "for the devotion I have lavished on you for four-and-twenty hours together now, or as near it as makes no difference?"

And before she could recover from her surprise at his audacity, he had placed his free hand under her chin, tilting it up slightly, and was just about to imprint a kiss upon her upturned face when an outraged voice behind them suddenly put an end to this romantic intention.

"Madam!" said the voice—Captain Belville's, as Gwendolen knew beyond the shadow of a doubt before she had even whirled round to face its owner, though it was shaking with such fury that it was almost unrecognisable. "Is this your—your *fidelity*?" he went on, in the tones of an admiral who has just witnessed flagrant insubordination in the ranks. "Have you quite forgot, madam, that you are promised to *me*?"

"Tut-tut, man," said Lord Wilfrid languidly, stepping

in to make matters worse before Gwendolen could speak, "don't, I beg you, have the bad *ton* to make a scene. What is a pic-nic, after all, without a flirtation?—and Miss Quarters is a devilish pretty girl, you know. Not a bit of harm in the whole affair—"

Gwendolen could see trembling upon the Captain's lips the retort of an honest man goaded beyond endurance by the condescending airs of a dandified libertine; but not even under the stress of seeing his betrothed in the embrace of such a one, she now realised, was he willing to extend to a duke's son the expression of the righteous wrath that he was only too willing to visit upon her.

"Sir—sir—!" he stammered stiffly. "I will leave to one side *your* part in this distressing affair! The matter lies between Miss Quarters and myself, and if you will be good enough to retire and leave us alone."

"With the best will in the world, my dear fellow!" Lord Wilfrid said obligingly. "I do so detest scenes, particularly before meals—highly upsetting to the digestion, don't you agree? But don't, I implore you both, be late to our little pic-nic luncheon. Victor—my papa's really excellent chef—assures me that he has quite outdone himself with the biscuit à la crème today. You will find us foregathering in no more than a quarter hour under that pretty pink muslin marquee you can just glimpse at the end of the alley. Miss Quarters"—with a polite bow—"your very obedient servant."

And he was gone, leaving Gwendolen to face unassisted the wrath of the indignant Belville.

But not so indignant, she saw in a moment, that he had not begun by this time to realise, with a great uplifting of spirits, that the most unwelcome scene he had so abruptly come upon meant Deliverance to him. Surely, his whole manner suggested as he began to speak, no man who had just witnessed his betrothed in the embrace of Another Man, and actually about to be kissed by him, need consider himself bound in honour any longer to marry her, regardless of what vows had been exchanged between them. It occurred to Gwendolen suddenly, and with considerable force, that if she did not wish to give the Captain the satisfaction of breaking off their engagement in all the glory of his own self-righteousness, she had best get down without delay to the business of dismissing him herself, so she raised one hand and said peremptorily, "Stop!"

Captain Belville, having been trained to take orders, did so without thinking, but then, recollecting from whom the order came, frowned and went on again.

"As I was saying—"

"You are not going to say anything, Henry," Gwendolen said politely but firmly, "until you have heard what *I* have to say." She hurried on, seeing the mutinous look upon the Captain's face, "In the first place, I must tell you how shocked and disappointed I am over your behaviour—"

"*My* behaviour!"

"Certainly, *your* behaviour. I had considered you a man of chivalrous impulses, a man upon whose noble nature I might rely to rescue me from the sort of disagreeable attentions forced upon me by Lord Wilfrid—

"Forced upon you!" The Captain's face grew red with disbelief. "But you came here with him yourself—!"

"Relying," said Gwendolen swiftly, with great aplomb, "upon his honour as a gentleman. How was I to imagine that he would take advantage of his own intimate

104

knowledge of the secluded nature of these gardens and my own entire lack of acquaintance with the place to which I was being led to press his attentions upon me? Or," she went on ruthlessly, as she saw the Captain again open his mouth to speak, "that the gentleman whom, of all others in the world, I had most reason to believe I could rely upon to protect me from him would, far from coming to my aid, instead place the most unmanly, low-minded interpretation upon the situation?"

"But, deuce take it, m-madam!" stuttered the Captain, struggling valiantly to get out of the corner he found himself fast being pushed into, "what else, I ask you, was I to think? You cannot deny that Lord Wilfrid has been pursuing you with his attentions ever since he first clapped eyes upon you last evening, and that you have given him no reason to believe that those attentions were displeasing to you —"

Gwendolen perceived that it was time to make her move, before the Captain had succeeded in pushing *her* into a corner.

"Captain Belville," she said, with an air of dignified regret which she felt that even Lady Otilia, a connoisseur of dramatic scenes, would have approved of, "you need say no more! I perceive, sir, that your long absence at sea has made you unfamiliar with the present usages of Polite Society, and that you are the sort of man who intends to behave disagreeably whenever the slightest occasion arises that may give him reason — however unjusti-fied — to believe he has cause for jealousy. Under such cir-cumstances, and with the greatest regret in the world, I must tell you that I think it best for us to part!"

"To part?" The Captain blinked at her, obviously torn between relief and indignation — relief at seeing freedom before him, indignation at having his role as the injured party reft from him. "Do you mean —?"

"Exactly," interjected Gwendolen, determined not to have the initiative snatched from her. "Our engagement, Captain Belville, is at an end. I believe a notice to that effect, placed in the *Morning Post*, may be called for, though, having no previous experience in this sort of situation, I cannot say with certainty. Perhaps you will be able to guide me?"

Captain Belville, almost choking now with his indignation over the insinuation that *he* might be the veteran of half a dozen broken engagements, managed to say with great acerbity that in this sort of thing he was quite as inexperienced as was she, after which they stood regarding each other inimically for several seconds and then, as if on a simultaneous impulse, began moving towards the pink muslin marquee at the end of the alley that Lord Wilfrid had mentioned. After a few paces, however, Gwendolen halted and turned to Captain Belville.

"I think," she said to him kindly, "I had best go first and you can follow in a few minutes, so that Miss Courtney will not think we have been quarrelling and say something witty and disagreeable about it. And it *might* help if you tried for a happier expression. Faces *are* so very revealing, you know."

Having said this, she went off down the long green alley, leaving Belville, almost stupefied by his emotions, behind her. To be freed of his obligation to marry a young lady who had no fortune and who he had had the direst premonition would make his life a burden to him with her blithe disregard for the proprieties on which he set such store was, it was true, a consummation devoutly to be wished. But to be calmly given his *congé* by her, to be patronised by her as if he had been a sulky schoolboy deprived of a treat—all this was extremely wounding to his dignity.

He walked slowly down the leafy alley, debating with himself how he ought to behave towards the infuriating Miss Quarters while they were obliged this afternoon to appear in public in each other's company. Should he act towards her in such a way as to make it clear to her that she had deeply offended him?—a pattern of behaviour which, he felt, might stand him in good stead when, as it was bound to, the awkward tale of the broken engagement would have to be told. Or should he strive to appear quite his usual self, a man whose conscience was clear and who was perfectly willing to behave with magnanimity towards the female who had used him so ill?

He could see that exasperating female's modish fawn-coloured gown fluttering on before him at the end of the long alley now, looking quite as carefree as if its wearer had not just been surprised *in flagrante delicto*—or at least in what passed in his mind as *flagrante delicto*—and then, abruptly, it halted and two other figures, one that of a tall, thin young man with a decided limp, the other that of a small young lady in a sprig muslin gown and a turban, came into view, just entering the alley at a rapid pace. The young man, it was true, had to labour to keep up with the young lady, handicapped as he was by his limp; but determination was in every line of his body, and he had no qualms, it appeared, against making use of an outraged, stentorian voice when he found the young lady outdistancing him.

"Cammie! Come back here!" he shouted furiously.

"I shan't! You're a *beast*!" the young lady called back,

halting for a moment to turn round in order to bestow this epithet upon him more vehemently.

Both young people, it was clear, were too occupied with themselves and each other to have yet taken in the presence of Gwendolen almost at the entrance of the alley or that of Captain Belville well behind her; and it was not until Campaspe, turning about again and resuming her flight from Lieutenant Fairhall, actually ran against her sister that she became aware that the scene in which she was so hotly involved was not being played out in private.

"Oh! Gwen!" she gasped, startled, but then went on at once, "How very *glad* I am to see you!" She turned about, clasping Gwendolen's arm tightly, her small figure very stiff and erect. "Will you kindly tell this—this *gentleman,*" she said, indicating young Lieutenant Fairhall with a gesture of superb hauteur, "that it makes me very happy indeed that he doesn't wish to be engaged to me any longer, because *I* do not wish to be engaged to *him*, either! And now—will you take me back to the others, please, for I most certainly do not intend to remain with *him*!"

Ten

To say that this announcement brought unalloyed dismay to the breasts of the several persons who heard it would be a quite inaccurate statement. Gwendolen, it was true, found it somewhat disturbing, though knowing her young sister, she thought the whole affair might well be a tempest in a teapot. But Lieutenant Fairhall was obviously far too angry to be dismayed by anything, and Captain Belville, it must be confessed, felt a sensation of unholy joy as he realised that the breaking off of his engagement to Gwendolen would be able to share the disagreeable light of public notoriety with the even more sensational rupture between young Fairhall and Campaspe.

He managed, however, to maintain his usual air of gravity, in spite of his elation, so that Campaspe, perceiving him standing rooted to the spot farther down the alley, and realising at the same time that Gwendolen had no intention of carrying her off until she had made enquiries into the state of warfare existing between what she had up to that moment considered a happily engaged couple, had no nesitation in walking up to him and saying, "Captain Belville, will *you* take me back to the others? I certainly do not wish to remain *here!*"

Captain Belville, who did not wish to remain there, either, but on the other hand had deep reservations about becoming involved in someone else's lovers' quarrel after just passing rather ingloriously, he felt, through one of his own, looked at her dubiously; but Gwendolen, who had walked on after Campaspe with Lieutenant Fairhall, resolved his dilemma by telling him to take her sister on to the marquee, as she wished to have a word with Lieutenant Fairhall.

"There is not the least use in your talking to *him*," Campaspe said loftily. "He is in an excessively bad temper and is *quite* unreasonable."

And she took the Captain's arm and walked off with him, leaving Neil fuming behind her.

"Look at her!" he gritted out. "Wouldn't you think, to see her, that *she* was the injured party? Actually, you know, she has been acting such an infernal flirt with Lyndale that there was no bearing it!"

"Yes, I know," said Gwendolen soothingly. "She has been behaving very badly—but it doesn't mean anything, you must realise. She is only young and thoughtless—"

Too dashed thoughtless for me!" Neil said bitterly. "But that's neither here nor there now, for our engagement is off, and it's nothing to me any longer what sort of May-games she takes it into her head to play!"

"Now, Neil, you *know* that is nonsense!" Gwendolen

said practically. "You and Cammie have been determined to marry each other almost since you were children, and you *can't* let some stupid little misunderstanding like this come between you now."

"Oh, can't I just?" Neil said wrathfully. He turned to her, the anger dying out of his face suddenly. "But I *am* a brute to come down on *you* with all this, Gwen," he said. "You're a good fellow—always have been—you're worth a dozen of Cammie! And I could see, by the look on Belville's face, that you already have trouble in that direction—"

"Not the least trouble in the world," Gwendolen assured him. "You may as well be the first to know, Neil, that Captain Belville and I have mutually agreed that we should not suit, so our engagement is now at an end."

Neil whistled. "Well," he said after a moment, frankly, "I can't say I'm surprised! Never did see how the two of you were going to deal together. I mean to say, a stiff-rumped man-milliner like that—!"

Gwendolen smiled a trifle ruefully. "No, really, you mustn't abuse the poor man!" she said. "I have the most lowering feeling that the whole affair was all my fault from the beginning: I simply couldn't stop myself, you see, from being Welsh and romantic about him, because I *adored* Lord Nelson, and then I *would* keep writing to him, so we got engaged. I don't suppose he ever really wanted to very much. But now he can go and marry Evelina Rutledge, at any rate, and I—"

Young Lieutenant Fairhall, who in the bruised and highly distressful state in which his quarrel with Campaspe had left him was feeling rather romantically dark and Byronic himself, here interrupted to say with boyish fervour that she was a Trojan to take it like that,

111

and that in his opinion Belville was dicked in the nob not to prefer marrying her to marrying Evelina Rutledge.

"Yes, but I haven't any fortune and she has, you see," Gwendolen said. "It is a great drawback to a female," she went on, glad to see that her companion had been diverted at least for the moment from his wrath against Campaspe, "not to have any fortune at all. For even though it appears to me that gentlemen who are already very well to pass ought to be able to marry for love and not for money, it seems that they are just as greedy as the rest. Not," she added fairly, as she began to walk on slowly down the alley towards the pink marques, "that *you* are greedy, Neil, and I do honour you very much for it."

Young Lieutenant Fairhall, feeling confusedly that he had never seen Gwen Quarters looking so beautiful and that here was someone who really understood him, not like that little cat Campaspe, said, with an unexpected sensation not entirely unlike intoxication, that the man who could place fortune in the balance against her love was not worthy of her affection, adding that he would marry her like a shot himself if he weren't already engaged. He then recollected that he was no longer engaged and flushed scarlet; but Gwendolen smiled at him very kindly and said not to be silly, because of course he was going to marry Campaspe.

"No, I'm not. I can't," he said gloomily. "She won't have me. She told me so. You heard her yourself." He added explanatorily and a trifle guiltily, "We had a most almighty quarrel. I'm sure Lyndale overheard us, and perhaps Miss Courtney, as well."

"Oh, dear!" said Gwendolen. "Well, you will just have

to make it up again, that is all. Here are the others. *Do* try to act as if nothing had happened."

They had come out of the yew alley by this time to the Great Garden, a series of parterres made in the French style and enclosing a long formal stretch of water leading to a small Palladian pavilion built in the manner of Batty Langley. Here the marquee to which Lord Wilfrid had alluded had been set up, and the other guests had already congregated. Gwendolen, seeing white napery, crystal goblets, and masses of silver, to say nothing of a perfect horde of servants and an orchestra in attendance, thought that it was a very odd sort of pic-nic; but she was relieved to find that, as everyone was busy eating and the musicians, inspired by the *al fresco* setting, were exerting themselves to the extent that conversation was almost impossible, she and Lieutenant Fairhall were able to merge into the scene with no particular notice being paid to them.

She was filling a plate for herself, having told Neil that under no circumstances must he think of waiting upon her, when she suddenly found Lyndale coming to her assistance.

"You are looking rather peculiar," he said to her. "So is Belville. Has anything happened?"

"What do you mean — has anything happened?" she parried cautiously, sitting down upon one of the French *fauteuils* that had been placed for the guests' comfort in the marquee, and that made it seem more than ever like an outdoor drawing room. She stole a glance at Captain Belville, who was sitting by himself, drinking champagne. There was certainly a rather addled expression upon his face, a kind of indignant-euphoric look, if the combination could be imagined.

"You know what I mean," Lyndale said, with his disconcerting habit of refusing to beat about the bush. "Look at the man. I know he went off after you and Wilfrid. What the deuce did you do to him?"

"*I* didn't do anything," Gwendolen said with dignity. "*He* did it. He found Lord Wilfrid trying to kiss me and said some very unkind things, so I told him we wouldn't be engaged any longer. I think he rather likes it—I mean, not being engaged."

Lyndale gave a shout of laughter.

"Don't do that," Gwendolen said reprovingly. "It isn't really very amusing. I mean, I came here today determined to tell him I wouldn't marry him, but still—"

"Not *wouldn't. Couldn't.*" Lyndale interjected. "And I told you so."

"Very well, then—*couldn't*," Gwendolen said coldly. "No *gentleman*, however, would say, 'I told you so,' to a lady."

"I've already informed you, I'm a bit out of practice," said Lyndale. "I'll apologise for the 'I told you so' if you like."

"Your apology," said Gwendolen magnanimously, "is accepted. After all, I daresay in a harem a man scarcely needs manners—"

"I regret to disillusion you, Miss Quarters," said Lyndale, "but, unfortunately, I must tell you that I never set up a harem. Not even a small one," he added, seeing a look of disbelief on her face.

"Well," Gwendelon conceded, "I expect it *would* be rather expensive. And perhaps you did not feel the need of a permanent establishment."

Lyndale, who was drinking champagne at the

moment, choked slightly. "That," he assured her, when he had recovered himself, "covers the situation very nicely, Miss Quarters. And now shall we return to *your* affairs? You were saying that you didn't find your dismissal of Captain Belville a subject for amusement—?"

"Well—not really," Gwendolen confessed. "*Not* that I think he is in the least unhappy about it, nor am I—but, after all, I had been used to being engaged for so long, and in love before that, and it feels rather strange to find I am not any longer."

"Yes, I expect it does. But you can always fall in love with someone else," Lyndale reminded her. "Girls do it all the time."

"*Not* if they are living at Brightleaves," Gwendolen said, shaking her head. "The neighbourhood is *very* thin of eligible men. I daresay that is why I fell in love with Belville. There *wasn't* a great deal of competition, you see."

"What about Wilfrid? He seems very much smitten with you."

"Oh yes, but I doubt that he would like to be engaged to me, much less married. Still, one never really knows. I don't suppose *your* friends expected you would wish to be married, either, a few months back."

"I'm quite sure they didn't. Would you like to marry Wilfrid?"

"What a very improper question!"

"And what a very evasive answer?"

"Well," said Gwendolen meditatively, "after all, he *is* a duke's son, and I expect I shall have to marry someone some day. But I *do* think I might do better—especially if I can persuade Aunt Pris to invite me to Brighton this summer. She was going to bring me out in London before she brought Jane out, you know, only I got engaged to Belville, so there didn't seem much point in it." She was interrupted by the sight of Campaspe, who had finished the large plate of food she had induced Captain Belville to bring her after they had arrived at the marquee, and was now making her way towards them, passing the chair in which Lieutenant Fairhall was sitting without bestowing so much as a glance upon him. "Oh, dear—here comes Cammie," she said. "*Could* you be very rude to her and send her away? You see, she has had the most dreadful quarrel with Neil Fairhall over you—"

"Yes, I know. I was privileged to hear most of it. Unfortunately, rudeness doesn't seem to serve with her; I've already tried that."

"Then I shall simply have to take her away myself. I *won't* have her creating another scene."

By this time Campaspe was upon them, smiling alluringly in Lyndale's direction. Gwendolen got up.

"Come along, Cammie," she said, firmly taking her younger sister's arm. "I want to talk to you."

"But I *don't* want—"

"Yes, you do," said Gwendolen, looking regretfully at her own half-finished plate. "And even if you don't, *I* do." She marched Campaspe off down the wide gravelled avenue, flanked with classical statues, in the direction of the white-columned pavilion at the end of the garden. "You have been behaving *most* improperly, you know," she said severely, as soon as they were out of earshot of the other guests. "Neil says you have broken off your engagement. That is a great piece of nonsense, of course."

"No, it isn't. I never want to see him again," Campaspe

said, putting up her chin. "He is the most un-reasonable —"

"It's not in the least unreasonable of him to disapprove of the way you have been throwing yourself at Lyndale's head. Cammie, you simply *must* put an end to that. You are doing Jane no good at all, and you are mortifying me to death by your want of conduct! And now it has come to breaking off your engagement. What on earth do you think Mama will have to say to that?"

"What do you think she will have to say to your breaking off *your* engagement to Belville?" Campaspe retorted. "You *have* done it — haven't you? He looked so Friday-faced that I made sure you must have. And if *you* can break off with him because he is pompous and disagreeable and you have found you don't love him any longer, why can't I do the same with Neil, when it is just the same with me and him? Oh!" She broke off, turning about suddenly, "I *thought* I heard someone behind us. It is Mrs. Webley and Mr. York. You *won't* mind if I leave you to walk with them, will you? I am dying to ask Mrs. Webley about the new hats she says are coming in; I thought I might trim up that old one of mine —"

And with this transparent excuse to avoid further scolding she ran off to join Mrs. Webley and her companion, who were just turning off into a secluded walk and would no doubt, Gwendolen thought, turn an exceedingly cold shoulder upon anyone coming to interrupt their tête-à-tête. Not, she was well aware, that that would in the least deter Campaspe, who had a fine disregard for the nuances of social intercourse, and was quite capable of talking millinery for half an hour together to two people who had had every intention of spending that same half hour in an agreeable flirtation.

She herself wandered on rather disconsolately towards the little pavilion at the end of the garden, conscious that she ought to go back to the others but smitten for the moment with a desire to be alone. It seemed to her that Life, which only a week before had been full of roseate plans and dreams, with wedding bells set to ring merrily and repeatedly in the near future, had suddenly become overcast and prickly with problems, if that was not mixing metaphors too badly. She was meditating gloomily on what she was to do about it when she became aware all at once that the little pavilion, which she had now got quite close to, was not deserted.

A graceful tableau, in fact, was being enacted there before her startled eyes — a set-piece as charming as that presented by the shepherd and shepherdess she had seen not long before leaning together in their delicate, statue'd embrace in the English garden. In the present case the shepherdess was a lovely, dark-ringletted young lady in an azure-blue gown, the shepherd a slim, fair young man in a well-tailored coat of Bath superfine — her sister Jane and Alain de Combray, without a doubt, though their faces were hidden from her behind one of the pavilion's chaste white pillars.

As she stood there, rooted in her place, a man's voice suddenly spoke behind her.

"A charming picture —"

She whirled about, speechless, to face Lyndale.

"It might," he continued, with every appearance of imperturbability, "have saved everyone a good deal of trouble, however, if I had had some notion of this sooner, Miss Quarters. Or was it this that you were trying so delicately to hint of to me the day I called at Brightleaves to make my offer?"

Into Gwendolen's head, as she stared, horror-stricken, into that bronzed, civilly impassive, yet surely, she thought, menacing face, dire visions rushed of two silent figures facing each other, right arms extended, gleaming pistols at the ready, in the dewy dawn of a summer's day on Paddington Green, or whatever might be the parallel spot in Gloucestershire to that convenient London rendezvous. She sought wildly for words, for some plausible explanation to palliate the cold thirst for vengeance that she was convinced must lie behind the cool, unreadable mask of Lyndale's face. Before she could speak, however, worse had occurred, for the lovers themselves, awakened from their dream of bliss by the sound of Lyndale's voice, had become aware that they were not alone. They sprang apart, twin blushes mantling their faces.

"My l-lord—!" stammered young M. de Combray, while Jane, unable to speak, buried her face despairingly in her hands.

It was a moment, Gwendolen saw, that imperatively required action of some sort, and though she had had no time to formulate a plan, she did the best thing she could think of under the circumstances, which to her romantically inclined mind included the certainty that Lyndale was about to flick his glove across Alain's face and say something like, "You will hear from my friends in the morning, sir!" Seizing his arm, she said to him forcefully, "You mustn't!"

Lyndale looked down at her in some surprise. "I mustn't what?" he enquired.

"Challenge him—to a duel!" Gwendolen explained desperately. And she went on, as a still more dreadful possibility occurred to her, "Or—or whatever it is that they do in Morocco!"

"Because Miss Jane has the good taste to prefer someone else to me? Don't be an idiot, Miss Quarters!" said Lyndale bracingly.

Jane, venturing to withdraw her hands from her face and to open her eyes at these astonishing words, stared at him imploringly, while young M. de Combray, upon whose delicate features red and white had fluctuated with alarming rapidity, took courage to draw himself up and say with all the steadiness at his command, "I—I fear, my lord, I owe you an explanation—"

"Nonsense! You owe me nothing of the sort," said Lyndale. "Miss Jane understands very well that she is bound by no promise to me—and I think I may well take advantage of this occasion to tell her that, if she wishes to, she may now release me from any promise that I have made to her. *If* she wishes to," he emphasised, looking directly at Jane, who, seeing his gaze upon her, once more covered her face with her hands and began to sob.

Gwendolen, who was herself so relieved by the entire lack of any murderous intent in Lyndale's words that she felt almost euphoric, went up and put her arms around her.

"Now *don't* be a goose, my dear!" she said. "It must be quite plain to Lord Lyndale that you have formed another attachment, and it will certainly be best if you tell him that you consider him free of any obligation to you—"

Jane's voice, muffled by sobs and by the fact that her face was pressed tightly against Gwendolen's shoulder, was heard to utter a few despairing words to the effect that she couldn't help it.

"No, of course you can't," Gwendolen said encouragingly. "But that doesn't get us any further, does it? You must just tell Lord Lyndale—"

"I can't! Mama!" the muffled voice made itself heard indistinctly once more.

Gwendolen started, and suddenly released her sister.

"Good God! Mama!" she, too, repeated blankly, as the overwhelming fact flashed into her mind that she would be obliged to face Lady Otilia, when they returned to Brightleaves, with not one, not two, but *three* broken engagements as the outcome of this fatal pic-nic. She looked at Lyndale. "See here," she appealed to him, "I simply *can't* tell Mama today that you and Jane have broken it off—*not* after I've just broken off with Belville and Cammie with Neil Fairhall. Would it make a *great* deal of difference to you if we wait a week or so before we tell people? I mean, you *don't* wish to get engaged to anyone else just at this very moment—do you?"

"At this very moment—no," Lyndale conceded, looking amused. "But it might be a good deal less embarrassing for everyone concerned, after all, if you would let Lady Otilia have your entire budget of bad news in one fell swoop, wouldn't it? We are all bound to be meeting constantly—which I feel might put more of a strain upon your sister's powers of dissimulation than they could well support—"

"Well—you *could* go back to London," Gwendolen suggested hopefully.

"By no means," said Lyndale, speaking with such emphasis that Gwendolen wondered suddenly if Miss Courtney had made more inroads upon his lordship's tenderer sensibilities than she, Gwendolen, would have believed possible, so that he was determined not to leave

121

Gloucestershire as long as she remained at Beauworth. He looked at Jane, who had stopped sobbing and was tragically regarding young M. de Combray. The latter at this point suddenly re-entered the conversation.

"I must tell you, my lord," he said, standing very erect and looking, Gwendolen admiringly thought, as gallant as any youthful aristocrat being drawn through the streets of Paris in a tumbril on his way to the guillotine, "that at the moment you came upon us, Miss Jane and I had been making what we considered our—our last farewell. I am in no position, *malheureusement*, to make her an offer of marriage—"

"My dears!" It was Miss Courtney's voice, trilling with laughter, that broke in upon this affecting scene and caused everyone involved in it to turn abruptly about with a variety of unpleasant sensations mirrored upon their faces. "How too, too naughty of me not to cough or say, *'Hem!'*—but I was so entranced by what I was hearing that I literally could not utter a sound!" She went on, to a stunned Jane, "I must say I really cannot blame you, my love—such a handsome boy, and the French are *tellement romantique*! But how distressing for *you*, Lyndale—!"

"Not half so distressing, Frieda," Lyndale interrupted her in a voice which both Gwendolen and Jane later admitted sent a cold chill down their respective spines, "as it will be for you if you repeat anything you have overheard here to any of your friends."

"Oh, dear! How *farouche* you *do* sound!" Miss Courtney said, making a quick *moue*. "But of course I shall be as silent as the grave!" she said, with such a total lack of sincerity that Lyndale looked grimmer than ever and Gwendolen thought in despair that any hope she might have had of keeping the matter from Lady Otilia was now completely at an end. Of course Miss Courtney, in spite of Lyndale's warning and her own extravagant promise, would spread the whole tale to her friends as fast as she was able to get back to them — and this she immediately proceeded to do, running off with a waver of her hand and a gay word to the effect that she was sure they wished to be alone.

"Detestable creature!" said Gwendolen indignantly. "You did your best, my lord, but I am quite certain that, even at the risk of displeasing you, she will still go at once and whisper every word she has heard to the Duke!"

"Yes, I think so," said Lyndale dispassionately. "As far as I know, there is no sure way to stop a woman's tongue, short of strangling her." He turned to Jane, who appeared to be still so stricken with a sense of her own guilt that she was unable to speak. "Well, that settles it," he said. "I shall go back to Brightleaves with you, and we shall see how your parents feel the matter had best be managed. You will have no objection to leaving now, I daresay?"

Jane said miserably that she wished very much to leave, and with a final heartrending glance at young M. de Combray, which Campaspe was fortunately not present to see, allowed Gwendolen to lead her away. Campaspe was collected, and in a short space of time three very subdued young ladies were being conveyed back to Brightleaves in the ducal barouche, with Lyndale riding beside it on a well-ribbed-up bay.

Eleven

Gwendolen spent the short period occupied by the drive back to Brightleaves in considerable dread of the scene she envisioned would be played out there when Lady Otilia received the news that all three of her daughters had once again been relegated to the role of unattached spinsters. She thought of the announcement she would be obliged to make as being more or less in the nature of a bomb to be cast into the peaceful, shabby drawing room; but what was her astonishment when, upon stepping across the threshold of that same drawing room, she found that the bomb — or at least a bomb of some sort — had apparently already been exploded there even before she had entered. For Mr. Quarters, with a face like a thundercloud, was striding up and down the long, sunlit apartment like a lion in a cage, uttering pithy expletives from time to time in place of angry roars, while Lady Otilia, seated on the somewhat dilapidated Chippendale sofa, appeared to be wringing her hands in the best tradition of theatrical melodrama.

"Papa! Mama! What in the world is the matter?" exclaimed Gwendolen, checking so abruptly upon the threshold that Campaspe, who was following directly behind her, almost fell over her.

Lady Otilia and Mr. Quarters, becoming aware that they were not alone, looked up and began speaking simultaneously, so that the four newcomers were greeted with a confused medley of words, from which only such salient phrases as "damned scoundrels," "ruined forever," and "never bear the disgrace" detached themselves ominously. Gwendolen, from whose head all thoughts of broken engagements had now departed, cast a glance of dismay at her sisters and went quickly across the room to seat herself on the sofa beside her mother.

"Now, Mama, *don't* cry," she urged, as Lady Otilia, at sight of her daughters, showed alarming signs of being about to burst into tears. She put her arms about her mother and looked up at Mr. Quarters, who had halted his pacing and now stood before the sofa, grimly surveying her. "Papa, *do* tell us what has happened to put you both in such a state!" she said. "You look as if the end of the world had come!"

"Aye, and so it has, my girl, as far as the lot of us are concerned!" Mr. Quarters said roughly, obviously controlling his temper only with the greatest difficulty. "We're being sold up. Those damned rascally cent-per-centers are foreclosing."

"Foreclosing?" Gwendolen stared up at him. She had lived for so long under the threat of a financial disaster that had always, by some minor miracle or other—a winning horse, a small legacy—been staved off at the last minute that she had grown used to believing that it would never really happen, and she could not in a moment adjust her thinking to the idea that it had now actually occurred. "But—but you *can't* mean we shall have to leave Brightleaves!" she expostulated.

"Oh, can't I?" retorted Mr. Quarters. "That's just what I *do* mean, and as soon as may be—and if those two scoundrels, Smith and Brown, think I don't know who is behind all this, they're fair and far off, I can tell you!" He stood looking down at her fiercely. "They have a buyer for the property, they say—a gentleman who wishes to remain anonymous," he said, with heavy scorn. "Well, he may wish to remain anonymous as much as he chooses, but *I'm* on to his little game! The Duke of Tardiff—*that's* his name and style, or may I never throw my leg over the back of a horse again!"

By this time Campaspe, Jane, and Lyndale were all in the room, attending to what was going forward there with varying degrees of interest and consternation. Lyndale, Gwendolen saw as she glanced up at him, looked as coolly detached as ever—as well he might, she thought with some resentment, since he was now free of his engagement to Jane. But Jane herself, whose natural forces were never of the strongest, appeared to be sinking entirely under this new shock to her sensibilities and, uttering a faint cry, seemed about to fall into a swoon except that Lyndale, quickly perceiving the situation, helped her to a chair.

"Oh, Jane, *don't* be such a noddy!" said her younger sister, not at all impressed by what she considered a piece of Londonish affectation. "What is there to swoon about, I should like to know? *I* shall not be in the least sorry to

126

leave Brightleaves. It is a dead bore, living in the country, and we shall have a famous time if we go to Cheltenham, as Mama is forever saying we must do if Papa is ruined—"

"In lodgings," Lady Otilia interpolated faintly, with a perceptible shudder. "I cannot bear it!"

"Well, I am sure we can be quite as gay in lodgings as anywhere else," Campaspe said stoutly, occupying herself in chafing Jane's hands and pinching her cheeks so briskly that her sister, in sheer self-defence, was constrained to give over all ideas of fainting and sit up. "There are balls and card-assemblies every evening during the Season, and the theatre, and the Pump Rooms, and *hundreds* of officers, even if half the people one meets there are the most dreadful old fogeys—"

Lady Otilia, looking outraged and tragical, said how could she talk in such a fashion when her family had just been reduced to beggary, and then, evidently becoming fully aware for the first time, in her distracted state, of Lyndale's presence in the room, said to him with great dignity, "Lord Lyndale! You will forgive me for having failed to greet you properly. The painful circumstances in which you find us—"

"Oh, there's not the least need to apologise; I understand perfectly, Lady Otilia," Lyndale said. He turned to Mr. Quarters, who was looking more than ever like an angry and frustrated lion, with his rufous face very much flushed and his sandy hair standing on end. "So Smith and Brown have given you notice they intend to come down on you," he said conversationally. "How bad is it, then?"

"Damned bad!" Mr. Quarters said with gloomy emphasis. "They can sell me up, lock, stock, and barrel, and, what's more, they intend to do it, the clutchfisted old squeeze-crabs! I told them I might be able to make a recover if they'd give me time—you know as well as I do, Lyndale, that I'm bound to have winners at Cheltenham Races with Conqueror and Dame Miracle—" He fell into a passion once more. "Damme, if it isn't more than a man can bear! My land, and my horses, too, to go to the Duke—"

"But it may not be the Duke who will buy them, Papa," Gwendolen interposed, leaving Lady Otilia to go and wind her arm persuasively through her father's. "After all, you don't *know* it is he your horrid Smith and Brown have in mind. And perhaps it won't come to anyone's having anything, after all. We have always managed to rub through somehow before, and I am sure we shall be able to do so again. Perhaps my uncle Horace will lend you enough to keep those creatures at bay—"

"Horace!" Mr. Quarters gave a contemptuous snort; it was well known that he had no opinion at all of Lady Priscilla's husband, who was enormously rich but had a fine attachment to his money that only his wife had ever learned the secret of overcoming. "It's not likely *he'll* come down with a groat; he told me last year, when he lent me a miserable monkey to stave off those blood-suckers, that I'd had the last of his blunt, and I'd sooner see us all in the poorhouse than go begging to him for more. But it won't come to that, I daresay," he concluded, gloom once more apparently overcoming wrath in his breast. "Your mother has a bit of money of her own, you know, and they can't touch that."

Lady Otilia, who in spite of Gwendolen's adjurations had got out her handkerchief and was weeping gently into it, was heard to utter a further despairing reference, in a muffled voice, to lodgings in Cheltenham. Mr. Quarters turned upon her irritably.

"Aye, in Cheltenham, ma'am!" he said. "I shall go there tomorrow and look out something suitable, for I won't stay here, I can tell you, to see my goods and chattels sold out from under me. And you may think yourself fortunate," he continued grimly, as Lady Otilia seemed about to utter a renewed protest to this scheme, "if it *is* in Cheltenham that we are able to settle, for it's far more likely we shan't be able to stand the nonsense there, either, and will have to flit to the Continent for economy's sake. They tell me living is very cheap in Boulogne."

"Boulogne!" Lady Otilia, suddenly abandoning her handkerchief, sat up straight and regarded her husband with an expression of passionate indignation in her prominent dark eyes. "No, *that* I will not do, Mr. Quarters, and there is an end to it! Go to Boulogne, indeed, and live in nasty damp lodgings, among foreigners! You need not ask it of me, for I will never do it!" She turned to Lyndale with an air of resolution. "Lord Lyndale," she said, "*you* must help us! I have been given to understand that your circumstances are such as to make it quite possible for you to do so, and surely you will not wish to see the family of the young lady to whom you are betrothed in such straits, when it is in your power to relieve them!"

Lyndale cast a glance at Jane, who had coloured up vividly and was looking at him imploringly.

"Unfortunately, ma'am," he said, quite with his usual imperturbable air, "your daughter and I are no longer betrothed."

"Yes, I know—not *formally*," said Lady Otilia, who

had apparently not taken in the full meaning of his statement, and assumed that he was referring to the fact that Jane had not yet given him her answer in form. "But it is all one—"

"No, Mama, it is not," said Gwendolen firmly, feeling it was time she took a hand in straightening out this embarrassing situation. "Lord Lyndale and Jane are not betrothed now, nor will they be in the future. Jane has formed another attachment, you see—"

"Another attachment!"

Lady Otilia stared incredulously at Jane, who looked for a moment as if she was again considering a swoon as the best way out of her dilemma. But beneath what her sisters tolerantly called her softness she, too, had a good deal of the family spirit, and, calling upon it now, she said to Lady Otilia in a reasonably steady voice, "Yes, Mama, another attachment. It is M. de Combray, and though I am quite aware that he is not at present in a position to ask me to be his wife, I am willing to wait—"

She was interrupted at this point by exclamations from both her parents, Mr. Quarters's consisting of—"De Combray! The devil you say!"—uttered in accents of decided displeasure, while Lady Otilia pronounced the words, "Merciful heavens!" in the tone of one who feels reason tottering upon its throne.

"You *cannot* mean to say," continued Lady Otilia in a quavering voice, "that you have been so *wicked*, Jane, so *ungrateful* for all the opportunities that have been given you—"

Gwendolen interrupted her. "Now, Mama, it will do no good at all to scold Jane," she said, "and, besides, it is not in the least her fault. She was saying good-bye to M. de Combray, just as you would have wished her to do,

130

when Lord Lyndale came upon them and divined the situation—and I am sure it will all be for the best in the end—"

"The best!" exclaimed Lady Otilia dramatically. "When she has made mice feet of our last opportunity to be saved from ruin!" A sudden inspiration seized her. "But no—not the last!" she went on, in a tone of renewed hope. "There is Belville! *He* is a man of substance; *he* will not wish to see his bride's family driven in disgrace from their home—"

"I am very sorry, Mama," Gwendolen said, with a sinking heart, for she foresaw the effect this announcement would have upon her mother, "but I am not going to be Captain Belville's bride." Lady Otilia stared at her wildly. "We have agreed that we shall not suit," Gwendolen went on, and then added hastily, to Campaspe, "Cammie, go and fetch Mama's vinaigrette—"

"Oh, very well," said Campaspe, who had the poorest opinion of people who found it necessary to have recourse to such remedies. "But you had best tell her at once," she recommended as she departed, "that Neil and I are not going to be married either, so she need not be saying next that perhaps the Fairhalls may help us."

She disappeared into the hall, and Lady Otilia, with a piteous moan, collapsed into Gwendolen's arms.

"Yes, I know, Mama—it is really very hard on you," said Gwendolen sympathetically, but without great alarm, for she knew that Lady Otilia's constitution was quite robust, and that, in spite of her liking for the dramatic effect, she was capable of sustaining the several unpleasant shocks she had just been obliged to undergo without any great injury to it. "But as Lord Lyndale has been saying to me, it is really better to have all the bad

131

news in one fell swoop, and get it over with." She looked up at Lyndale, who, unlike most men when faced with an emotional scene in an acquaintance's drawing room, was exhibiting no signs of a craven desire to escape, but instead appeared to be taking a great interest in the whole proceeding. "I expect you wouldn't care to come to the rescue with a nice large loan, even though you are *not* to marry Jane?" she asked him hopefully. "I am quite sure you can afford it—"

"Oh yes, I can afford it," Lyndale agreed. "The question is, can Miss Jane?"

"Jane?" Gwendolen looked at him uncomprehendingly. "But what has she to do with it?"

"Well, for one thing, she might feel obliged to marry me," Lyndale pointed out. Gwendolen began to speak, but he cut her off. "Miss Jane," he reminded her, "has, as I have discovered, a very well developed sense of duty. Now who is to say that, if I come down with a considerable sum to save Brightleaves, she won't feel it her duty to forget young M. de Combray all over again and marry me?"

This, Gwendolen was obliged to admit, was an unanswerable question. Jane, faced with such generosity and, moreover, with the strong opposition of both her parents to her entering into any sort of understanding with Alain de Combray, was only too likely to be led to reverse the decision into which circumstance had forced her today and agree to wed Lyndale, after all. Lady Otilia, however, who obviously took an entirely different view of the situation, here revived sufficiently to say in an accusatory voice to Lyndale that she would have thought that *that* was exactly what he desired.

"As for M. de Combray," she said superbly, "I am sure

132

you must know that young girls are always having these kinds of romantic fancies. I myself was desperately in love with my dancing master before I married Mr. Quarters. It signifies — I may tell you — nothing."

Gwendolen was a good deal taken aback at hearing her mother utter such heresy against the romantic point of view to which she had always been a strong adherent; and it was obvious that Campaspe, re-entering the room at that moment with her mother's vinaigrette, was equally surprised.

"But, Mama, how can you say such a thing?" she objected. "You have always told us that one should never marry except from inclination — "

"And so I say still," said Lady Otilia with some asperity, rejecting the vinaigrette with a wave of her hand, "but what there is about Lord Lyndale to disgust any female I am sure I cannot conceive! It is true that his complexion is very brown, but no doubt residence in England will remedy that in time: and I most certainly have not the least notion why Jane cannot have an inclination for him if she will only put her mind to it — particularly since by doing so she will be able to save her entire family from ruin!"

Gwendolen, who, though used to her mother's habit of speaking with extreme and often embarrassing frankness when her emotions had been called into play, was not at all certain how Lyndale would take this mixed encomium upon his appearance, gave him a questioning glance, and was relieved to see that he seemed to have accepted it quite calmly. Mr. Quarters, however, who had been holding himself in with bit and bridle, so to speak, while all these revelations of broken engagements and their disagreeable consequences were being debated, here exploded and said with great bitterness that in his opinion a man was a fool to have daughters; and with this Lear-like statement he stamped out of the room and was shortly to be heard calling vehemently for one of his horses to be saddled.

"You must forgive him, Lord Lyndale," said Lady Otilia, who appeared to have quite got over any idea of swooning away and was now sitting very upright upon the sofa, like a plump but determined hen who has made up her mind to look after her chicks properly even if they have all turned out to be ducklings, and ugly ones at that. "Men *do* have such a tendency to become angry when it will least serve—*not* that you are not a man your-self, so you will know exactly what I mean. But I am very happy to see that *you* are not angry, which I am sure is greatly to your credit, with Jane behaving so very foolishly, so if you will be so kind as to sit down here beside me, I believe we may well be able to sort this mat-ter out—"

She looked hopefully at Lyndale, but to her disap-pointment he did not respond to her appeal, but only stood gazing down at her with what she considered a highly enigmatic though, at the same time, somehow reassuring smile.

"I think not, Lady Otilia," he said. "But if I were you, I should try not to worry about it too much. You still have three very attractive daughters, and who knows that one of them may not end up a marchioness, after all? Ladies, I bid you all good-day!"

And with a comprehensive bow he walked out of the room, leaving Lady Otilia glowering after him.

"*Odious* man!" she said. "As if marquises were as plen-tiful as gooseberries in Gloucestershire! He will marry that encroaching Miss Courtney, I have not the least doubt, and Belville will marry Evelina Rutledge, while as for Neil Fairhall, he will undoubtedly turn into one of those men exactly like his father, who never think of marrying anyone, because they are far too busy with their hounds and their horses, until they have reached the age of five-and-thirty, and by that time Campaspe will have been on the shelf for years!" She bent a sybilline gaze upon her three abashed daughters. "I see," she said, "that *I* shall have to Take a Hand in affairs, for obviously I have raised three daughters with more hair than wit, who have not the least notion as to where their best interests lie! I shall have Pris here from Brighton at once, and between the two of us we shall see if we cannot settle you respectably in spite of yourselves!"

Twelve

True to her word, Lady Otilia sent an express off to her sister that very day, with the result that Lady Priscilla, in a ravishing carriage dress of French green and a matching bonnet with an audaciously curtailed poke, arrived at Brightleaves before the week was out. She swept into the house, paying no more heed to the packing cases that were already littering the hall than if they had been the conventional tables and ornaments ordinarily to be found there; and, presenting her cheek to Lady Otilia, who had come out to greet her at the sound of carriage wheels, went at once with her into the drawing room, where she sat down with great aplomb on a sofa upon which a large family portrait was already reposing.

"Now, my dear Otilia," she said, "you will be good enough to tell me at once everything about this ridiculous situation you have got yourselves into. Lodgings in Cheltenham, indeed!—and *three* broken engagements! I vow I don't believe there is another family in Christendom that could have got itself into such a hobble!"

Lady Otilia, who was the elder of the two by several years, but who had never, since childhood, been able to get the better of her tall, rather gauntly slender, decisive sister, gazed at Lady Priscilla a trifle rebelliously, but then, realising her desperate need of help, said meekly that it was not her fault.

"Of course it is not," Lady Priscilla said, taking off her gloves and bonnet. "It never is. Hugh is *quite* unmanageable; I have known that ever since you married him. But that is neither here nor there," she went on, charitably consigning Mr. Quarters and his shortcomings to consideration under less urgent circumstances. "The chief point is, what are we to do about those girls of yours? I will admit I was not all surprised to hear that Campaspe had broken off *her* engagement, for she has very little sense and even less conduct. But I should have expected better of Gwendolen, who is sensible enough to be aware that, at one-and-twenty, she cannot afford to be too nice in her requirements. Captain Belville, I understand, is a very respectable *parti* for a girl with no fortune, and I shall attempt to impress that fact upon her."

Lady Otilia said rather gloomily that she might spare herself the trouble, for Captain Belville had not lost so much as four-and-twenty hours in making up to Evelina Rutledge, and was already to be seen parading the High Street in the village with her on his arm, quite in the style of an engaged man.

"But," she went on, brightening slightly, "Lord Wilfrid Boulting has been calling almost every day, and obviously to see Gwendolen, so I *do* think there may be some hope in that direction."

"Wilfrid Boulting?" Lady Priscilla looked skeptical. "Oh, I shouldn't place too much reliance upon *him*," she said. "He must be very much *épris* indeed to make an offer of marriage to any female. I must warn you that a score of caps have been set at him, and some by diamonds of the first water, which you yourself will be the first to admit dear Gwendolen is *not*."

Lady Otilia, who was very fond of her eldest daughter, said a trifle indignantly that Gwendolen had a great deal of originality. Lady Priscilla waved a dismissive hand.

"Yes, I know, my dear — but originality is *not* what most men are looking for in a wife," she said. "In point of fact, if she were to strive for a little less originality it might be easier for us to get her off. But is there no other *possible he* except Lord Wilfrid?" she went on. "Of course I *could* take her to Brighton, but young men at fashionable watering-places so often think only of amusing themselves, and those who are more serious are usually fortune-hunters and wouldn't be interested in her in the least."

Lady Otilia said a trifle doubtfully that there was Neil Fairhall, who was also a great deal at Brightleaves, oddly enough, since he and Campaspe had broken off, ostentatiously ignoring his erstwhile betrothed and talking for hours to Gwendolen when she would let him.

"Of course he *is* a year younger than she is," she said, "but I daresay that doesn't signify. And, really, if Campaspe has been foolish enough to let him get away, it does seem only fair that Gwendolen should have him. She has always liked him very much."

Lady Priscilla said briskly that they might at least consider him a possibility, and then brought up the subject of Jane's behaviour vis-à-vis *her* betrothed.

"I think I may say," she remarked, "that I was never more shocked in my life than when I read in your letter that she had jilted Lyndale—which is what it comes to in the end, even though they were never officially engaged. Such a pretty-behaved girl she seemed in London! I should never have believed she could do anything so wicked as to turn her back on a marquisate and fifty thousand a year! I saw at once, of course, that *I* should have to have a talk with her."

Lady Otilia, bristling a little at this criticism of her middle daughter, in spite of her own similar feelings upon the subject, said it wouldn't do any good, because Lord Lyndale had suddenly taken it into his head to go back to London, and had obviously no intention of marrying Jane now.

"That odious Miss Courtney has been on the catch for him ever since he arrived in Gloucestershire," she said, "and now that he has returned to London she has suddenly discovered she must go there, too—in July, my dear, when of course there is no one in town but Cits and mushrooms!—and I have no doubt she is contriving to see him. I expect the next thing we shall hear is that *they* are engaged."

Lady Priscilla, however, refused to take such a gloomy view of the situation, declaring that Frieda Courtney was not at all the kind of young lady that Lyndale had given her to understand he was looking for in a bride, and adding that if she and Lady Otilia put their heads together, they might yet succeed in making a match of it between him and Jane.

"Depend upon it," she said, "he is not the kind of man

to stand upon his dignity and take offence because of a girl's having a passing fancy for a handsome young man, and I have no doubt that if we can bring Jane to see the folly of her pining over a penniless Frenchman, who has no prospects whatever of being able to marry her, we may yet bring the Lyndale affair to a successful conclusion."

She then, being a woman of boundless energy, expressed a desire to be driven into Cheltenham so that she could see for herself the small house there in which Mr. Quarters proposed to settle his family. Gwendolen and Campaspe, arriving home at that moment from the village, whence they had accompanied Jane, who with her usual good nature had offered to spend the afternoon with a very deaf old lady whose niece-companion was obliged to be absent during that time, were at once included in the party, even though they would gladly have declined the honour, being well aware that Lady Priscilla would occupy the drive to Cheltenham in scolding them for their very improper behaviour in breaking their engagements.

However, they were rewarded at the end of the drive by the opportunity to examine their new home. It was a tiny house with a bow-windowed drawing room giving on one of the less imposing terraces of the thriving spa, and would have done very well for a small young couple beginning married life in a modest way, but appeared appallingly cramped to Lady Priscilla and Lady Otilia for a family that included three very lively young ladies.

But if the two elder ladies shook their heads forebodingly over the small drawing room, the three tiny bedrooms upstairs, and the servants' quarters up still another breakneck flight of stairs, with their oval windows almost entirely blocked by the low parapet that ran round the roof, Gwendolen and Campaspe were delighted with the prospect of living in a terrace that looked more like a wedding cake than a street, with its lacy frills of delicate ironwork and its elegantly pilastered façades. Nor was their enthusiasm tempered by the sight of the constant flow of traffic visible from the bow-fronted drawing room — modishly attired ladies in sedan chairs, strolling officers, fashionable tilburies and four-in-hands dashing over the stones, gouty gentlemen and invalidish spinsters on their way to the Pump Rooms, or to Bettison's or Williams's Library. Campaspe had at her fingertips a catalogue of all the gaieties the town provided — balls on Mondays and Fridays, cards and the theatre on Tuesdays, Thursdays, and Saturdays, a dress card assembly held on Wednesdays — and declared her intention of attending every one of them.

And then there was the prospect of Race-week, if they were fortunate enough to complete the move from Brightleaves by that time, when the hotels would be crammed with visitors, and balls, routs, races, and plays would offer an endless variety of amusements and opportunities to three young ladies in search of husbands.

Even Lady Otilia, who was inclined to take the darkest view of everything at the moment, was obliged to agree that such opportunities would be far more numerous in Cheltenham than they had been in the comparative seclusion of Brightleaves, if only the eligible gentlemen who were to be found in that fashionable spa were willing to overlook the dismal state of the family finances that had confined them to such cramped quarters. And she was even brought to admit at last that the drawing room, though small, was quite elegant, with its *chinoiserie* wall paper and frail chandelier.

The party was therefore able to return in a tolerably cheerful mood to Brightleaves, where they found Mr. Quarters just come in from a farewell tour of the stables, for his horses were about to be sent off to Tattersall's on the following morning. He was in a melancholy-mad humour, ready to be inflamed upon the least provocation into a quarrel with his sister-in-law, whom he cordially disliked, and dinner was accordingly enlivened by a highly acerbic conversation between the two, during which the shortcomings of each were unsparingly discussed by the other. Meanwhile, Gwendolen and her sisters, not anxious to have the battlefield artillery turned upon themselves, sat silent in a row, as prim as church-mice. This, however, did not save them—Jane, in particular—from having their duty pointed out to them after dinner by Lady Priscilla in the baldest of terms, with the result that Jane was soon reduced to tears, Campaspe to fierce scowls, and Gwendolen to a most unseemly fit of the giggles.

"I can't help it," she defended herself later that evening to Campaspe, when they were alone together. "The very thought of my following Aunt Pris's advice and 'attempting to attach Belville again,' as she puts it, is enough to send me into whoops. The poor man was so pleased to be rid of me that I expect he would run as if the devil were at his heels if I gave him so much as a come-hither look. As for Neil Fairhall, if she could overhear our conversations, she would understand perfectly well that the only reason he comes to see me is to talk about you and how badly you have behaved towards him."

"Well, he has behaved just as badly towards me," Campaspe said hotly. "He said I was an infernal flirt and he didn't care to be married to me, and when I tried to explain to him that I was doing it all for Jane, he wouldn't listen to me. And speaking of Jane," she went on, characteristically forgetting her displeasure almost as soon as she had given vent to it, "I think we shall have to do something about her again. She is weakening; did you see her face when Aunt Pris was telling her what a wicked, ungrateful girl she was for not snapping up Lyndale the moment he made her the offer, and how it was all her fault that we are obliged to leave Brightleaves?"

"Yes, but there is nothing she or anyone else can do about it now, with Lyndale in London," Gwendolen said practically. "Even Aunt Pris can't expect Jane to pursue him there, and I should think it highly unlikely that he will return to Gloucestershire in the near future. He is certainly not on the most cordial of terms with the Duke or Lord Wilfrid, and now that he has broken off with Jane, there can be no reason for him to visit this part of the country again."

She was somewhat surprised to find herself attacked by a twinge of regret as she spoke these last words, a twinge that she attributed, upon consideration, to the fact that, in spite of the really outrageous candour of his conversation—or perhaps because of it—his lordship could be counted upon to enliven to a notable extent any gathering at which he was present. Certainly there could be no other reason for her regretting his absence from Gloucestershire!

It was an emotion that was soon forgotten, at any rate, in the bustle of the family's removal to Cheltenham, which was complicated even further, in her case, by the fact that Lord Wilfrid Boulting and Lieutenant Neil Fairhall were constantly underfoot, each of them appearing to be quite willing to overlook the disorder of a house people were just moving into or out of in order to obtain the pleasure of her company. It was a new experience for her to be so pursued, and though she had the gravest suspicions that the goal of neither of her suitors was honourable matrimony, she could not but be somewhat flattered by all the attention she was receiving. Lord Wilfrid had already claimed the privilege of escorting her to one of the balls to be held during Race-week at the Assembly Rooms, and Neil had booked rooms at the Plough in Cheltenham for the sole purpose, he said, of being at her service to gallant her to any of the Race-week festivities in which she wished to participate.

All this was heady stuff, and if only, she thought, Jane were in better spirits, they might all enjoy themselves famously during Race-week and forget about the vexing question of finding three eligible gentlemen who were willing to marry them.

Or at least so she thought until Campaspe burst in upon her during the first morning of Race-week, as she was busy trimming a gypsy hat of Lady Priscilla's with ribbon of a colour more suitable for a young lady of one-and-twenty than for a matron of two-and-forty, and plumped herself down in a chair opposite her with an expression upon her face indicating that she was pregnant with ominous news.

"You will never guess," she said impressively, when she could catch her breath, for she had run up the stairs at top speed, "who I've just met in the High Street!"

"Whom," said Gwendolen automatically and somewhat absently, holding the hat up to inspect it critically. "Cammie, do you like this ribbon? I rather thought —"

"Oh, what do I care for ribbons!" Campaspe interrupted, with violent impatience. "Do you know who—*whom* I've just met? Lyndale! In the High Street! He's come back!"

"Lyndale?" There was no further question now of the hat; it dropped upon the small work table beside her as Gwendolen stared at her sister. "Here? Oh, you must be mistaken!" she said disbelievingly.

"How could I be mistaken when he spoke to me?" Campaspe said scornfully. "He's here, I tell you—and, what's more, he asked me where we were living now and said he meant to call upon us at once. I ran all the way home so I could warn Jane. I expect that's him now," she added, as a confused noise in the hall below resolved itself into the agitated tones of their very young maid endeavouring to cope with a male visitor. "Well! He hasn't wasted any time, has he?" She leaned forward and spoke urgently to her sister. "Gwen, we shall have to *do* something, don't you see?—for he has certainly changed his mind about Jane and has come back to make her marry him!"

Thirteen

It was the merest curiosity, Gwendolen told herself,
and certainly no desire upon her part to see the Marquis
of Lyndale again, that sent her downstairs to the drawing
room with Campaspe a few minutes later. They found his
lordship in amiable conversation with Lady Otilia, Jane,
and Lady Priscilla, who was not staying at the house,
owing to its cramped accommodations, but fortunately — at least from her point of view — had arrived
shortly before from her rooms at the Royal for the purpose of discussing plans for the day. Jane, it was true, was
taking very little part in the conversation, but sat, with
the half-demented but very appealing look on her face of
the wronged heroine in a coloured ballad-sheet, gazing
down at her hands, which were tightly clasped in her lap;
but her mama and her aunt more than made up for her
silence with their own excessive cordiality.

"Disgusting!" said Campaspe in Gwendolen's ear as they paused together on the threshold, and without further ado she marched across the room and dragged up a chair between Lyndale's and Lady Otilia's, upon which she sat with somewhat unnecessary emphasis.

"Good morning to you again, Lord Lyndale," she said. "You certainly haven't let the grass grow under your feet—have you? Have you come to ask if you may escort us to the races today? Lord Wilfrid has offered to gallant us, but I do think three females are too much for any man—don't you? So if you like, *you* may excort *me*, and leave Lord Wilfrid with only Gwendolen and Jane."

During this speech, which had been uttered very rapidly and with great determination, Lady Priscilla and Lady Otilia had been regarding her with undisguised shock and disapproval, obviously restraining themselves with difficulty from ordering her to go to her room at once and telling her that she should have no supper. But Lyndale appeared quite unperturbed by her advances.

"I should be delighted," he said politely, but with an enigmatic glint that might, Gwendolen thought, have been amusement or something rather more disquieting in his eyes. "That is," he added, "if you don't think Wilfrid will object."

"To you gallanting *me*? Oh, no, it is Gwen he is dangling after," Campaspe said, upon which both Lady Priscilla and Lady Otilia exclaimed, "Campaspe!" in tones of strong disapproval. "Well, it's true!" Campaspe maintained stoutly. "Not," she continued, once more turning to Lyndale, "that we think he wishes to marry her, for Aunt Pris says he is not a marrying kind of man, but one never can tell, can one? And at least he is very useful in squiring her around."

147

Lyndale, who was looking at Gwendolen, which for some reason made her wish to look anywhere but at him, said that in his experience a young lady of Miss Quarters's strength of character who wanted to be engaged to a man usually succeeded in her object, upon which Gwendolen stopped not looking at him and regarded him indignantly.

"If you are referring to Captain Belville, my lord," she said, "he *did* wish to marry me. He wrote and asked me to."

"Yes, but that doesn't prove he *wished* to," Lyndale said amiably. "I daresay, if the truth were known, you had manoeuvred the poor fellow into such a position that he couldn't do anything else." Gwendolen gasped. "No, don't rip up at me," Lyndale said, grinning. "I am sure you could do the same with me, if you set your mind to it. But you have had no thoughts along that line, I expect?"

"Considering," said Gwendolen, mastering her wrath and speaking with excessive coldness, "that until recently you have been all but contracted to my sister, my lord, I may truthfully say that I have not! Nor," she added, growing even more furiously polite as she realised that, in the face of the startled and disapproving attention of her sisters, her mother, and her aunt, she was colouring up scarlet, "*nor*, may I say, should I have been tempted to do so even had the circumstances been quite different!"

"Yes, I can understand that," Lyndale said, apparently not in the least abashed by what she had meant to be a crushing set-down. "I'm not easy to make into a romantic figure, like the gallant Belville, though I assure you I do my best. All that Moroccan business, for example—I expect some men might make a very good thing out of that with the ladies. But the only person I seem to have succeeded in impressing is your father. *He* finds my Arabian mares very romantic."

"Mr. Quarters," said Lady Priscilla definitely, for she felt that this highly unorthodox conversation had gone quite far enough, "has not a romantic bone in his body, Lord Lyndale! And," she added, with an air of resignation, as the front door of the little house was suddenly opened and shut with a violence that set every crystal drop of the drawing-room chandelier dancing, "speak of the devil, as the saying goes —! Here he is now, I make no doubt!"

She was quite correct in her surmise: the next minute the drawing-room door had been flung open and Mr. Quarters appeared upon the threshold with an expression of such wrath upon his highly flushed face that even Lady Priscilla was momentarily taken aback. His eyes swept the small room, lighting up fiercely at the sight of Lyndale seated there at his ease between Campaspe and Lady Otilia.

"Hah!" he exclaimed, as dramatically as even Lady Otilia could have done. "So you're here, are you, Lyndale? Under *my* roof! Of all the infernal gall —!"

"But why," enquired Lady Priscilla, rising to the occasion and speaking with her usual practical good sense, "shouldn't Lord Lyndale be here, Mr. Quarters? He has come to call upon your wife and daughters — an eminently proper attention to pay them, it appears to me, showing that he bears no ill will because of Jane —"

"Jane! What has Jane to say to it?" Mr. Quarters demanded, his fury not a jot abated by these calming words. He strode farther into the room and, stationing himself directly before Lyndale's chair, glared down at him with an unwinking stare. "As for bearing ill will," he continued, addressing the company at large but continuing to glare at Lyndale, "why the devil *should* he bear ill will to anyone, when he's succeeded in carrying out the lowest, most underhanded piece of business—"

"Mr. Quarters!" Lady Otilia interrupted, in tones of the greatest shock. "Remember that Lord Lyndale is a guest in your house!"

"Well, *I* didn't ask him here," Mr. Quarters retorted rudely, but with perfect truth. "And if he likes to step outside, I'll show him that I ain't too old yet to teach him a lesson he won't forget—"

"What is it, Quarters? The horses?" Lyndale, who seemed not at all put out by his host's singular lack of cordiality, enquired with a grin. "But someone had to buy them up, you know. That's why they were sent to Tattersall's."

"Yes, that's why they were sent there!" Mr. Quarters agreed wrathfully. "To be bought up—but *not* by some jumped-up marquis who came nosing around my stables to spy out what he could, and then, when he saw he was on to a good thing, refused me a loan and went sneaking off to London to get my horses into his own hands! I'd as soon Tardiff had them! Sooner!" declared Mr. Quarters, who was rapidly working himself into a passion and, if left to himself, would no doubt presently have consigned his horses with great good will to the devil himself, rather than have them fall into Lyndale's hands.

"But what can you be thinking of, Mr. Quarters," Lady Priscilla here interrupted incredulously, "to be making such a piece of work over it because Lord Lyndale—as I gather from your *most* intemperate remarks—has bought your horses? Obviously you could not afford to keep them yourself, so what possible difference can it make to you whether Lord Lyndale has them or someone else?"

"He is racing them!" Mr. Quarters gritted out, still confronting Lyndale. "Here! At Cheltenham!"

"Well," said Lyndale unblushingly, "I rather thought you'd like to see them run, you know. What's more, I'd say your Conqueror has a good chance to come off with the honours—"

"He's not *my* Conqueror! He's *yours!*" said Mr. Quarters, refusing to be mollified by this praise of an animal that had been foaled and trained under his eye. "And I hope," he added, to show the extent of his present alienation, "he may come in dead last! I hope they all will!"

"Now, Papa, you know you don't mean anything of the sort," said Gwendolen, who considered that matters had now gone far enough. "You would be mortified to death if anything of the sort happened."

"No, I wouldn't!" said Mr. Quarters recalcitrantly. "And what's more, I won't have such a sneaking, underhand fellow marrying my daughters! Any of them! Do you understand that, Lyndale?"

And he glared once more at the Marquis.

"As to that, Mr. Quarters," Lady Priscilla reminded him disapprovingly, "there has never been a question of his marrying any of them but Jane, and if Lord Lyndale should be so condescending as to renew his suit to her, I am sure that even you will not be so foolish as to stand in her way."

But Gwendolen, moving swiftly—for she foresaw that if her father were to engage Lady Priscilla as well as Lyndale in verbal warfare, there would be no end to the battle—tucked her arm through her father's and, saying persuasively, "Come along, Papa," led him fuming out of the room and into the dining room, where she poured out a large glass of Madeira from the decanter on the sideboard and handed it to him.

"Drink that and you'll feel much better, Papa," she said consolingly. "It *is* quite odious of Lord Lyndale to have bought your horses behind your back, but after all, if he hadn't, the Duke would have done it, which would have been quite as bad."

Mr. Quarters, in no mood for consolation, said unforgivingly that it wouldn't have been, because he knew where the Duke stood and he had considered Lyndale a good fellow and a friend; but he consented to drink off the bumper. He then, with some further animadversions against marquises, and an adjuration to Gwendolen never to marry any of them, because he wouldn't have one of them in the house, took himself off to meet, she suspected, with some of his racing cronies and discuss Lyndale's traitorous behaviour with them over some further spirituous consolation at the Plough or the George, leaving her free to return to the drawing room.

Here she found that Neil Fairhall had joined the company and was engaged in ignoring Campaspe quite as pointedly as she was ignoring him. He professed himself greatly disappointed upon learning that Lord Wilfrid had been before him securing the honour of escorting Gwendolen and Jane to the races that day, but Lyndale said encouragingly that, as he himself was to gallant Campaspe, he would be happy to have Neil join *their* party—a suggestion that was greeted with frigid silence by Campaspe, and by young Lieutenant Fairhall, after a glance at her haughtily averted profile, with a flush and a hastily muttered excuse.

152

"You can see for yourself," Campaspe said vengefully to Gwendolen when Neil had gone off with Lyndale shortly afterwards, "that you are *quite* wrong in thinking that Neil wants to make it up with me. He comes here to see *you*, not *me*, and if you would like to marry him, I am sure I shall not have the least objection. In point of fact," she went on, with an air of resolution, "I have had the most splendid idea: it came to me when Papa said he wouldn't have Lord Lyndale marrying any of his daughters. Why should *I* not marry Lyndale? Then he will be obliged to do something for Papa, just as if he had married Jane, and we shan't have to go and live in Boulogne, and Jane will still be free to marry Alain—"

But here Gwendolen interrupted her with a sharpness that surprised her almost as much as it did Campaspe.

"Oh, *don't* be such a widgeon, Cammie!" she said. "As if Lyndale would think of such a thing—!"

"Why shouldn't he think of it?" demanded Campaspe, stung. "I know I am not as beautiful as Jane, but everyone says I am quite well-looking—"

"Yes, and I expect you think you are as docile and well-conducted as Jane!" said Gwendolen dampingly. "You *are* a widgeon, Cammie! Lyndale would no more consider marrying you than he would think of marrying me—and heaven knows we have been coming to cuffs ever since the day we first met!"

"Well, he doesn't come to cuffs with *me*," Campaspe said indignantly. "We get on together famously, and I daresay we should deal extremely if we were married. It won't do any harm to ask him, at any rate."

"To *ask* him! Cammie, you *wouldn't*!"

"Well, not *precisely*, perhaps," Campaspe admitted, a

little daunted by her own audacity. "But one *can* always lead men on."

"Well, I *don't* see how you could lead him on any more than you have done already," Gwendolen said, somewhat relieved — and then, after Campaspe had flounced out of the room, asked herself what on earth she had had to be relieved about. Certainly she, Gwendolen, could have no objection to Campaspe's marrying Lyndale if she could bring him to the point. Such a marriage would, as Campaspe had pointed out, solve all their problems without sacrificing Jane to a loveless marriage, and if she, Gwendolen, was such a dog in the manger as to begrudge her young sister a brilliant marriage because she herself had no present prospects of marrying anyone at all, she deserved to pass the rest of her days as a spinster.

So she spent the next hour in a mood of violent self-dislike, which for some reason appeared to include a violent dislike of Lyndale as well, whom her father had no doubt been perfectly justified in referring to in terms of the greatest disapprobation. All of which did not prevent her from spending that same hour in feverishly removing all the lavender ruched velvet ribbon that trimmed the charming figured French muslin dress Lady Priscilla had given her to wear that afternoon, and replacing it with pale-blue ribbon less trying, she felt, to the complexion. She was doing it, she told herself, to impress Lord Wilfrid. What Lord Lyndale might, or might not, think about the substitution was, she also told herself loftily, a matter of the most complete indifference to her.

Fourteen

The Cheltenham Races were held on Cleeve Downs, and thither Gwendolen, Jane, and Campaspe, all appearing in their best looks in their pale summer frocks and wide-brimmed hats, were escorted by Lyndale and Lord Wilfrid, the former driving his curricle and the latter a smart barouche. It was a fine, warm day—perhaps too warm, with a threat of rain in the heavy white clouds showing their thundery-blue undersides against a bluer sky. But the sunshine gleamed richly now on the procession of carriages, horsemen, and foot-travellers of every description thronging the road to the Downs, and Gwendolen was determined to forget, at least for a few hours, all the vexing problems besetting her family and enjoy herself.

This, she soon saw, would not be difficult to do if she enjoyed flirtation, for Lord Wilfrid was at his most *galant*, and obviously had every intention of providing Jane with other suitable company as soon as might be possible, with a view towards having her, Gwendolen, to himself. Gwendolen wondered if he might even be preparing to propose marriage to her, for there was an odd, significant intentness in his manner towards her that she had never observed there before. Like a very large, self-satisfied white tom-cat preparing to pounce on a mouse, she thought idly, regarding Lord Wilfrid's pale, supercilious profile as he tooled his team of matched-greys expertly through the jostling traffic on the crowded road—after which it suddenly occurred to her that the tom-cat, in such a situation, had something more predatory than courtship on his mind.

Was she indeed about to receive an improper proposal from Lord Wilfrid? Of course she knew she ought to be highly insulted at the very thought, but the truth was that she felt it would be a great deal easier for her to handle that sort of thing than an offer of marriage, which would leave one in a most uncomfortable dilemma between duty and inclination. She certainly did not wish to marry Lord Wilfrid, but on the other hand he was a highly eligible *parti*, especially for a portionless young lady of the advanced age of one-and-twenty, and she had a lowering feeling that she would be almost as indecisive and generally birdwitted as Jane had been about Lyndale in trying to make up her mind whether to have him or not.

"Of course I *ought* to, if it is really marriage that he offers me," she told herself, "for I haven't Jane's excuse of being in love with someone else"—but even as she said the words to herself, a face quite unlike Lord Wilfrid's pale, complacent one flashed into her mind, a deeply bronzed face with intensely blue eyes, a determined chin, and a mouth that could curl into an arrogant but likable grin.

And what had Lord Lyndale to say to the matter? she asked herself in something of a temper at her own unaccountable silliness in thinking of him at such a time. Obviously, nothing at all, for it was quite clear that, in spite of his rather improper remark earlier that day about her being able to make him offer her marriage if she wished to do so, he had not the least interest in the eldest Miss Quarters, and on the contrary considered her to be a disagreeable and "overmighty" female, certainly not at all the sort of person one would wish for a wife.

All of which for some reason caused her, when they had reached the Downs and Lord Wilfrid's barouche had by an unlucky chance been drawn up beside Lyndale's curricle, to give her escort far more encouragement than she would ordinarily have done if there had been strangers seated beside them. When they arrived, the area was already crowded with dozens of other carriages, drawn up three and four deep, generally without horses, and many of the occupants were discussing pic-nic nuncheons, while all around them the colourful hangers-on at such festivities plied their trades. A troupe of brightly clad gypsies was staging a display of acrobatics while their women climbed up into the carriages to have their palms crossed with silver and read the fortunes of the occupants; Mr. Punch in his booth engaged in raucous battle with Judy; minstrels chanted "The Roving Soldier" or "The Westbury Cocking"; and around the white betting-post, a hundred paces from the goal, a dense throng of bettors—earls and dukes, grooms and livery-servants, "sharpers" and "black-legs"—shouted out their wagers, making such a din that it seemed impossible any business could be transacted in it.

Jane, always timid in the midst of a large, boisterous crowd, shrank back into a corner of the barouche, scarcely tasting the cold chicken, the creams, aspics, jellies, and champagne produced in lavish abundance from a large hamper by Lord Wilfrid's groom, and regained some animation only when Campaspe, who had eaten enough for a young lady twice her size and had had a lively dispute with Lyndale, ending in total defeat, over the question of her being provided with a glass of champagne, announced her intention of having her fortune told.

"Oh no, Cammie—indeed you mustn't!" she said earnestly as her young sister, almost falling out of the curricle in her efforts to attract the attention of one of the gypsy women, beckoned her to the carriage. "You know what dreadful thieves those people are—"

"Well, I haven't anything to steal, and I daresay Lord Lyndale is rich enough to afford another watch if they prig his," Campaspe said. She smiled brilliantly at the dark, gaily shawled young woman who had come up to approach the carriage. "Here is my hand," she said, offering it to her. "If you tell me a splendid fortune, I am sure Lord Lyndale will cross your palm with twice as much silver as he will if you tell me a horrid one. Shall I be married soon, or go on a journey?"

The gypsy took her hand and studied it intently.

"Oh, very soon!" she confirmed almost at once, looking up at Campaspe with an enigmatic smile. "Very, *very* soon! *And* go on a journey—"

"Good!" said Campaspe, giving a little jump of satisfaction and excitement. "Is he fair or dark! Is he"—she shot a mischievous, meaningful glance at Lyndale " — at all like this gentleman?"

The gypsy, who obviously saw how the land lay, shrugged noncommittally.

"Who can tell?" she said evasively.

"Well, *you* ought to be able to tell," Campaspe answered her downrightly. "It's what you're being paid for, isn't it?"

The gypsy, without replying, abandoned her hand and cast a quick, sidelong glance up at Gwendolen.

"And you, pretty lady—?" she said in a wheedling voice. "I can tell a fine fortune for *you* if the gentleman'll cross my palm with silver."

"By all means," said Lord Wilfrid lanquidly, drawing a half-crown from his pocket. "What sort of fortune would you like, my dear Gwen? A dark stranger and a trip across the water? Yes, I think definitely a trip across the water, but perhaps one could omit the dark stranger. A fair gentleman with whom you are already acquainted might serve the purpose even better—"

While he had been speaking, the gypsy had been scanning Gwendolen's palm, and at these last significantly uttered words she suddenly glanced up at Lord Wilfrid with a sly, derisive smile.

"Aye, *serve the purpose*—that's the word for *you*, fair gentleman," she said impudently. "Mayhap you'd like me to read *your* palm, sir? It might save you a deal of trouble."

"No, I want none of your mumbo-jumbo," Lord Wilfrid said coldly. "You may earn your silver by reading the young lady's palm, and predicting the usual fate of health, wealth, and a long, happy married life for her."

"Aye, long," agreed the gypsy, again glancing at

Gwendolen's hand, "and happy, but,"—looking up into Gwendolen's face—"stormy, pretty lady, stormy. You'll marry the best, but you'll give him no rest—and you'll travel far countries with him—"

"Oh, how exciting it sounds!" Campaspe exclaimed. "*Much* better than mine!"

"Excitement enough for the pair of you, miss," said the gypsy obligingly, and let her slanting gaze slide up to Lyndale's face. "And you, dark lord," she said to him as impertinently as she had spoken to Lord Wilfrid, "shall I tell you *your* fortune?"

Lyndale grinned down at her. "I have an idea," he said, "that you already have—haven't you? Here—"

He tossed her another coin and she scrambled down from the carriage and melted into the crowd.

"Now *what* did you mean by that?" Campaspe demanded. "She wouldn't say if the gentleman I am to marry is dark or fair, or if he is at all like you, so she can't have meant—"

"Never mind what she meant," Lyndale said. "What I mean to do is to take you to the Duke's marquee, where we shall have a better view of these races. You have eaten quite enough, and Conqueror will be running soon."

Lord Wilfrid at once said that he would escort his ladies there as well, but Jane, who cared nothing for the races and was disinclined to brave the crowd in order to make her way to the marquee, said if he did not mind she would merely move to the carriage on their other side, which was occupied by some old friends with whom she had spoken during the nuncheon, and remain there instead. Lord Wilfrid, scarcely troubling to conceal his satisfaction at this—for him—fortunate turn of events, assisted her with alacrity to her new place and then bore Gwendolen off in triumph.

"How perceptive of your sister to leave us alone, fair charmer — I *may* call you fair charmer, mayn't I?" he drawled, as they made their way through the crowd. "I am feeling very seventeenth century today, you see."

"Oh no, I don't mind," Gwendolen said, unfurling her sunshade and wondering if one could have an improper proposal made to one while strolling through a crowd of this magnitude. "I should quite adore to look seventeenth century myself, with my hair all in tight curls like Queen Henrietta Maria and a spaniel in my lap, but I'm afraid I am dreadfully modern at heart. I mean, if anyone were to call me Sacharissa, I should probably go into whoops."

"So you say," murmured Lord Wilfrid in a lower voice, placing his free hand over the hand with which she lightly held his arm as they walked along and pressing it significantly. "So you say, fair charmer. But would you actually be more averse than any seventeenth-century damsel to being swept off your feet by a dashing cavalier and carried off across his saddle-bow?"

"A very uncomfortable mode of transportation, I should think," said Gwendolen in a perversely prosaic tone. "A nice, smart, modern phaeton would be much more the thing."

"Then a phaeton it shall be, my dearest Gwen," Lord Wilfrid interrupted, neatly cutting the ground from under her feet and speaking almost in a whisper in her very ear. "You *do* understand me, I think? You *will* come? By the happiest of chances, my noble papa's yacht is even now lying convenient at Bristol, equipped for a cruise and entirely at my disposal. I so long to show you

161

Venice—yes, I think it must be Venice for you. A palazzo overlooking the Grand Canal—"

"Good heavens!" exclaimed Gwendolen, stopping dead in her surprise, thus causing a stout gentleman in a blue coat with brass buttons walking immediately behind her to tread upon the heel of her sandal. A profusion of exclamations and apologies followed, during which Lord Wilfrid so intimidated the stout gentleman with a bored, bleak stare that he broke off in the middle of his explanations and scurried off like a rabbit.

"The poor man!" said Gwendolen. "And it was really all my fault, you know, for stopping so abruptly! But I could not help it; you took me so much aback with that absurd speech. I was almost thinking that you meant it!"

"But I *did* mean it," said Lord Wilfrid, stung into an unusual show of animation by this crass misunderstanding of his romantic intentions. "My dearest girl, since I first saw you, I have thought of nothing else—"

"Really? I should think *that* would have been a dead bore," said Gwendolen amicably. "But I *know* how it is when one gets an idea into one's head—"

"What I meant to convey," said Lord Wilfrid, rather between his teeth, for it is difficult to make a declaration of passion in the midst of a crowd to a young lady who persists in misunderstanding you, "is that I adore you, and I want you to go away with me! At once!"

"What—in the middle of the races, and leave poor Jane to find her way home alone? Really, Lord Wilfrid—!"

"When I say *at once*," said Lord Wilfrid, his pale face unwontedly tinged with colour, for he did not like to be thwarted and even less did he like to be laughed at, "I mean tonight—tomorrow—whenever it may be convenient to you. I am entirely at your service—"

"Well, if you are, you will stop talking nonsense about my going away with you," Gwendolen said decidedly. "Of course I shall do no such thing, Lord Wilfrid. Good gracious, I think you must have had too much champagne! At least that is the only excuse I can think of for your having made such a very foolish suggestion! Oh, there is the Duke!" she went on, as His Grace of Tardiff, supported on either side by Miss Courtney and Lady Maria, made his way slowly from the marquee which, in total disregard for the rights or rules of anyone else, he always had erected for himself conveniently near the finish line. "How do you do, My Lord? I do hope I find you well."

The Duke, after looking her over from head to foot and remarking in a lecherous aside to Lord Wilfrid that she was a demned fetching piece, said he was never well and asked her if her father was satisfied now.

"Satisfied about what?" Gwendolen enquired, quite at a loss.

"About getting the better of me over his horses — *and* his land," said the Duke, almost with a snarl, as Gwendolen later described it to Campaspe. At that moment Campaspe herself came up with Lyndale, and the Duke went on, addressing Lyndale with an exceedingly ungracious air, "I wonder *you* have the face to show yourself here, sir! Very clever you and Quarters think yourselves, no doubt, to have put the change on me!"

"Oh, Quarters had nothing to do with it, Duke," Lyndale said, with an agreeable smile. "In point of fact, he told me himself only this morning that he would far rather *you* had his horses."

"*And* his land, I expect!" the Duke said, with heavy scorn. "Trying it on much too rare and thick, Lyndale; I have more sense in my knowledge-box than to swallow *that* fling! You're going to marry his daughter, ain't you?"

"Oh, well—that remains to be seen," said Lyndale —enigmatically—upon which Campaspe cast a significant glance at Gwendolen. "But you mustn't believe, at any rate, Duke, that you are the victim of a deep-dyed plot of his," Lyndale continued. "The point is merely that my offer to Smith and Brown was better than yours."

The Duke grunted, still much dissatisfied, it seemed, and Gwendolen, who had been standing quite lost in astonishment at the revelations contained in this brief exchange, found herself being led to a chair by Lord Wilfrid, who had not the least interest in what happened to Mr. Quarters's land *or* his horses, and was bent upon demonstrating to her his extreme displeasure over the highly unsatisfactory manner in which she had received his amorous advances.

But if he had been the Prince Regent himself, Gwendolen would not have noticed the studied hauteur of his manner towards her, so great was her surprise over the information that had just been conveyed to her by the conversation between Lyndale and the Duke. It was Lyndale, then, and not the Duke, who had bought up Brightleaves from Messrs. Smith and Brown!—and why he should have done so, unless, as Campaspe suspected, he was still determined, in spite of everything, to marry Jane, she simply could not conceive. He might well have wanted her father's horses for himself, as Mr. Quarters had accused him of doing, but he could not, she thought, have wished to purchase Brightleaves for any other purpose than to oblige his future father-in-law and prevent the estate from falling into the hands of strangers. But if this were so, why in heaven's name had he not declared his action openly to Mr. Quarters?

Even the excitement of the races, the cheers of the spectators, and the satisfaction of seeing Conqueror come in a winner (diminished though that satisfaction might be by the fact that his jockey was wearing the silks of the Marquis of Lyndale instead of the Quarters colours) failed to distract her mind from the questions that had been raised in it. She *might*, of course, ask Lyndale directly what his motives had been, for he sat beside her during the better part of the races, observing with some amusement, it seemed to her, Lord Wilfrid's frosty demeanour and her own rather *distrait* manner; but somehow she could never seem to think of the right words in which to phrase her questions. And, at any rate, Campaspe, who had suddenly developed a highly confidential air with her escort, was monopolising his attention almost completely. Was it really possible, Gwendolen asked herself in bewilderment, that it was Campaspe, and not Jane, whom Lyndale intended to marry? He was certainly showing no annoyance now over her proprietary airs, but even seemed to be encouraging her.

She returned to Cheltenham, with Lord Wilfrid and Jane, in a fever of impatience to question her father, and see if he might be able to throw some light at least upon the perplexing matter of Lyndale's purchase of Brightleaves.

"Papa, did you know that it is Lord Lyndale who has bought up Brightleaves?" she asked him the moment he entered the hall of their small house just before the dinner-hour, after she had lain in wait for him there ever since her own return.

Mr. Quarters stared at her, his heavy brows beetling over his blue eyes.

"Lyndale? Pooh-pooh, girl!" he said brusquely, after a moment. "You don't know what you're talking about"—and went to walk past her to the stairs.

Gwendolen seized his arm. "But, Papa, it's true!" she insisted. "I heard him talking to the Duke this afternoon, and it is he who has bought Brightleaves, not the Duke!"

A rather singular expression, which appeared to his daughter to be compounded of annoyance, guilt, and a certain quite unaccountable smugness, came over Mr. Quarters's face.

"Pooh-pooh!" he said again, but even more unconvincingly. "I don't believe a word of it! Why should Lyndale wish to buy Brightleaves? You must be all about in your head, my girl!"

And he walked on up the stairs, leaving Gwendolen to gaze after him in frustrated indignation.

"But perhaps," she said to herself, as she followed him slowly up the narrow staircase, "he is so angry with Lyndale already that he can't bear to think of his having Brightleaves, too, and that is why he won't believe it. I don't know *what* he will do if he hears that Lyndale still wishes to marry Jane—or, worse still, Cammie! Oh dear, I *do* wish none of us had to marry anyone! It is all such a muddle, for I am quite sure that Cammie doesn't care tuppence for Lyndale, and is still as much in love as ever with Neil, if only the two of them weren't too stiff-necked to admit it!"

All of which led her to remember that young Lieutenant Fairhall was to escort her to the ball at the Assembly Rooms that evening, where no doubt she would be obliged to meet Lyndale and Lord Wilfrid as well and where the whole perplexing and distracting problem of who was to marry whom, or in Lord Wilfrid's case run off with whom, would no doubt come up again. It was a daunting thought, and only the consideration that she would be wearing a distractingly becoming dress of Lady Priscilla's that evening gave her sufficient courage to face it.

Fifteen

Gwendolen had been so much involved with the questions aroused by her afternoon at the races that she had scarcely noticed that Campaspe and Jane had also returned from their excursion to Cleeve Downs in rather peculiar moods. In Jane's case, the peculiarity took the form of retiring to her bedchamber and indulging in a bout of tears, due, Campaspe remarked, to her having seen Alain de Combray at the races; but, as Campaspe also observed, fortunately Jane had the happy ability to cry her eyes out without ruining her face, so it really didn't matter about her being such a ninnyhammer just before a ball.

As for Campaspe, *her* peculiarity consisted in the adoption of an air fraught with so much deep mystery and dark importance that it would have aroused curiosity in a statue. Gwendolen had an uneasy notion that it all had something to do with Lyndale, and wondered what new plans her young sister had concocted for setting them all by the ears; but Campaspe, for once, remained mum when she threw out a few inviting leads for an exchange of confidences, and at any rate there was really not much time for that sort of thing in the bustle of preparing for the ball.

Jane was to wear cornflower-blue, always her best colour, with a draped tunic *à la romaine*; Gwendolen had been made happy with the presentation to her by Lady Priscilla (who had been obliged to return to Brighton temporarily) of a water-green sarsnet gown with a deep, square-cut neckline and the short, puffed sleeves known as *bretelles*; while Campaspe gloried in a frock of marigold-yellow, and had crimped her curls in the Caracalla style, faithfully copied from the current number of *La Belle Assemblee*, which she had carefully studied in Duffield and Weller's Literary Saloon.

To Campaspe's further triumph, Lyndale had offered to escort her to the ball, and he completed her felicity by presenting to her a posy of yellow-and-white hyacinths, with their stalks tightly encased in silver paper and tied up with long ribbons. Gwendolen, obliged to cope with young Lieutenant Fairhall's unlucky choice of mauve and purple blossoms, was relieved of the necessity of wearing them by the arrival, just before she left for the ball, of a spray of yellow roses in an elegant holder, the accompanying card bearing the cryptic words, *Je persévère*.

"Oh, dear! Lord Wilfrid, of course!" she said to Neil. "Do you mind very much if I don't carry either your flowers *or* his this evening? I'm afraid I was rather rude to him this afternoon—*not* that he didn't thoroughly deserve it!—and he is certain to feel dreadfully snubbed if he finds I have chosen your posy instead of his."

Neil, who had arrived just in time to see Campaspe mounting triumphantly into Lyndale's carriage, said rather gloomily that he didn't mind in the least, and proceeded to prove it by bursting into what he apparently believed to be a gay, entertaining monologue upon his lack of good fortune at the races that afternoon, where every horse he had backed seemed to have come in last.

Unfortunately for the effect he was attempting to create, he frequently lost the thread of his anecdotes completely, stopped dead, and appeared to become absorbed in his own thoughts, from which he would presently wrench himself with a sudden start.

"Good gracious," said Gwendolen, when this had happened for the third time just as they arrived at the Assembly Rooms, "what *is* the matter with you this evening, Neil? You act as if you were planning to commit murder and weren't sure you had the plot straight."

To her surprise, Neil coloured up scarlet and, looking quite as guilty as if she had indeed divined his horrid secret, stammered in an exculpatory voice that he had been thinking.

"Yes, I know you were," Gwendolen said. "But about what? You haven't been called back to the army, have you? I don't think your leg is nearly well enough yet."

Neil said no, that wasn't it, and looked at her so imploringly that she immediately, having heard of the ways of young men, surmised that he had either (a) been badly scorched in one of Cheltenham's gaming establishments, or (b) become entangled with one of the many

170

fashionable and charming Birds of Paradise who flocked there during Race-week.

In either case, she had no wish to embarrass him by plying him with further questions, so she kindly began to talk about what a crowd there already seemed to be in the Rooms, and said that if he wished to find a place to sit down, he had best look round at once, or he might be obliged to stand all evening.

"Perhaps you might like to go upstairs to the card room, or the billiard room," she said. "I shall do very well now; there is Jane, with her prosy Mr. Williams—I *do* think it is odd, since she is so very beautiful, that only the dullest young men seem to wish to gallant her—and I shall join them, or— Oh, here are Cammie and Lord Lyndale," she said, as her young sister, who had apparently entered the room just before them and was preening herself under the attention her arrival with Lyndale had attracted, came rapidly towards them.

"Oh, Gwen," she at once said, looking straight through Lieutenant Fairhall as if he were a pane of glass, "I have told Lyndale that he must stand up with you for the first set because of the person you came with not being able to. *I* am going to dance with Mr. Clurton, and then Lyndale can stand up with *me* for the second set, so that's all right."

And she flew off across the room, leaving Gwendolen to stare after her with a slight frown upon her face.

"She is looking very odd," she said to Lyndale rather accusingly, after a moment. "Almost as if she were about to burst with excitement. What in the world have you been saying to her?"

Lyndale said readily but not quite convincingly that he had said nothing at all.

"At least nothing to make her burst," he said. "I think you are allowing your imagination to run away with you, Miss Quarters. She seems quite her usual self to me."

"No, she isn't," Gwendolen insisted. She looked at Neil. "Perhaps it was you that made her look so queer," she said, "because you didn't even say good evening to her" — and then halted suddenly in astonishment, for as she had turned to regard Lieutenant Fairhall, she had surprised him in the very act of directing a look of anxious, conspiratorial interrogation at Lyndale. Whatever it was that had the young lieutenant in such a state of mental ferment that evening, it was now obvious that it had something to do with Lyndale, but she could not conceive in what way the two could have any matter of importance in common. A dozen improbable conjectures chased themselves through her head: among them that Neil had lost money at the gaming-tables to Lyndale — that he was unable to pay; that he and Lyndale were involved in an illegal conspiracy to fix the results of tomorrow's races; and, worst of all, that he had quarrelled with Lyndale over the latter's attentions to Campaspe and had engaged himself to fight a duel with him in the morning.

The last of these conjectures seemed to her, on the whole, the least improbable of the lot, and her anxiety that it might be true caused her to say downrightly to Lyndale, as he led her into the set, "What is the matter between you and Neil? Have you been quarrelling with him?"

He turned an amused face upon her. "With young Fairhall? What in heaven's name should I quarrel with him about?"

"I don't know," said Gwendolen, regarding him closely. "Cammie, perhaps? You seem to be growing very particular in your attentions to her!"

"Do I?" Lyndale enquired, without, she noted, a flicker of surprise or self-consciousness. "Still, I can't see why that should concern Fairhall. *He* has obviously set his sights upon *you* now."

"Oh, *don't* be idiotish!" said Gwendolen impatiently. "You can see as well as I can that he is still head-over-ears in love with her, and is only making up to *me* so that he can continue to see *her*. And I *do* think," she went on severely, "that it is too bad of you to interfere, and puff her up with expectations that you have no intention of satisfying!"

She looked into his face as she spoke, in order to see what effect her words would have upon him, and was somewhat surprised to note that, for once, there was an unwanted expression of faint perturbation in his lordship's eyes.

"You don't mean," he enquired abruptly after a moment, "that she really does want to marry me, Miss Quarters?"

Gwendolen stared at him. "Well, that is a very odd thing for you to say!" she exclaimed. "I should have thought, from the way you have been making up to her, that it was your endeavour to bring her to that point!" Her own eyes suddenly kindled dangerously. "Do you mean to tell me, my lord," she demanded, "that you have been amusing yourself at that child's expense? I must say, I should have expected better of you!"

"Well, I should rather have thought the shoe was on the other foot myself," Lyndale said, "but if you mean have I any serious intentions concerning your young sister, Miss Quarters, I assure you that I can relieve your mind upon that score."

She cast a fulminating glance at him, but nevertheless felt herself fortunate that the movement of the dance separated them at that moment, for she felt that the conversation had somehow got into deep waters and that she had no notion how to go on with it. On the one hand, she was furious with Lyndale over the casual manner in which he had denied that his attentions to Campaspe had any serious meaning; and on the other she was very much relieved that such was the case, for she certainly did not feel that Campaspe's future happiness lay in marriage to Lyndale. By the time she and his lordship came together again, the conflict between these two points of view had become so severe that she could scarcely speak civilly to him, which did not seem to disconcert him in the least. As soon as the set was at an end, Campaspe appeared beside them on the arm of Mr. Clurton and, dismissing the latter, bore Lyndale off.

"I *do* wish," said Jane in gentle anxiety, also appearing beside Gwendolen at that moment on the arm of her Mr. Williams, "that Mama had not had the headache this evening, or that Aunt Pris had not been called back to Brighton! I know it is quite respectable for you, at your age, to have charge of Campaspe, but, really, she pays not the least heed to you, and the way she is behaving towards Lord Lyndale this evening quite puts me to the blush!"

"Yes, I know; there is no doing anything with her," Gwendolen said, "and he is quite as bad, for encouraging her. Oh, Mr. Williams," she added hastily, as she saw Lord Wilfrid bearing down on her through the crowd with an unwontedly purposeful air, "*will* you be so very kind as to stand up with me for this next set? You see, I particularly do *not* wish to dance with Lord Wilfrid Boulting."

Mr. Williams, after a moment of appearing a good deal taken aback by this highly unconventional application, said with grave gallantry that he would be honoured; Jane looked shocked; and Gwendolen, reflecting resignedly that Jane probably thought her behaviour quite as unbecomingly forward as Campaspe's, turned to face Lord Wilfrid.

"My dearest Gwen—" he said, bowing low over her hand and then raising it to his lips with a peculiarly significant smile. He added, in a deeper, injured tone, "You are not wearing my roses—my peace-offering, so to speak—"

"No—no, I am not," Gwendolen agreed, a trifle disjointedly. "You see, Neil—Lieutenant Fairhall—expected me to wear *his*, and as I couldn't oblige both him and you, I am wearing neither."

"Indeed!" said Lord Wilfrid, only partially mollified. "But I hope this does not mean, dearest Gwen, that I am not forgiven. The violence of my feelings—"

Gwendolen, uncomfortably aware that Mr. Williams, who could not leave because of his engagement to dance with her, could overhear every word Lord Wilfrid was saying, and disbelieving utterly, at any rate, in Lord Wilfrid's having any violent feelings whatever except for those of an overweening *amour propre*, said rather unkindly that she supposed everyone said things they didn't mean sometimes and walked off with Mr. Williams.

But after having been bored almost to tears by the lat-

175

ter gentleman's laborious conversation and awkward partnering in the dance during the ensuing set, even Lord Wilfrid's company seemed less disagreeable to her, and she was almost resigning herself to standing up with him for the next set, as she saw him approaching her across the crowded room, when a servant suddenly appeared at her elbow and addressed her.

"Begging your pardon, ma'am — but would you be Miss Quarters?"

Gwendolen acknowledged that she was and, in some surprise, saw the man produce a folded note and hand it to her.

"Lord Wilfrid, of course!" she thought at once, as the man moved away and she unfolded the note, though why Lord Wilfrid should have troubled to write to her when he had every opportunity to speak to her that evening, and indeed seemed bent upon doing so at the present moment, she found it difficult to guess.

But the moment she had unfolded the note, she saw that she had been entirely mistaken in her surmise. It was Campaspe's sprawling schoolgirl hand, not Lord Wilfrid's dashing one, that leapt up at her from the page, and by the time she had perused the first sentence, Lord Wilfrid had gone completely from her mind — which was scarcely surprising, for by then she was already frozen with horror.

Dear Gwen, the brief missive read, *By the time you read this I shall be gone off to marry Lyndale. Don't fall into a pucker, or let Mama do so, as I am sure you will both agree that this is the best way out of all our difficulties. Pray pack up my best things and send them to the White Hart in Bath, though Lyndale says not to trouble because he will provide for me, but I should like to have my new Pamela bonnet. Campaspe.*

Mechanically, Gwendolen refolded the note and pushed it into her reticule, her mind in such a mad whirl that she was only vaguely conscious that Lord Wilfrid was now standing before her and was addressing her with his usual meticulous courtesy.

"I—I beg your pardon!" she exclaimed, almost at random. "I was not attending, I fear! Such a vexatious thing—someone has trodden upon my gown and torn the lace! Will you excuse me?"

And she walked off quickly towards one of the small anterooms that opened from the ballroom, leaving Lord Wilfrid staring after her with an expression of great affront upon his face.

She *must*, she felt, be alone for a few minutes so that she could think what to do! Fortunately, the room was empty, and, sinking down into the nearest chair, she took Campaspe's note from her reticule and spread it out to peruse it once more.

By the time you read this I shall be gone off to marry Lyndale—and yet within the hour she, Gwendolen, had had it from Lyndale's own lips that he had no serious intentions towards the child! Odious, abominable man! It was bad enough for Lord Wilfrid, who was known throughout the *ton* as a cynical man of the world, to offer a *carte blanche* to a young woman of one-and-twenty, who had certainly cut her eyeteeth and would be well aware of the risk she would be taking if she accepted it. But for Lyndale, under the guise of offering honourable matrimony, cold-bloodedly to seduce a girl just out of the schoolroom was conduct so infamous as to choke her with

177

rage. She *must* stop him, and by the greatest of good fortune, owing to Campaspe's childish infatuation with her new Pamela bonnet, she knew exactly where to come up with him — but how was she to get to Bath?

Of course, the most obvious solution was to ask Neil to take her home at once, tell her father what had happened, and rely upon him to go after Lyndale.

"But no — good God, that will never do!" she thought at once, horrified. "He would be sure to call Lyndale out, and I should have his blood upon my head!"

The idea of applying to Neil was as quickly negatived for the same reason, for certainly she could no more depend upon the impetuous young soldier merely to rescue Campaspe without becoming embroiled in a quarrel with her seducer than she could upon her hotheaded father.

"I shall simply have to go after her myself!" she thought in despair. "But how? I haven't more than five shillings with me, and even at home I haven't enough by me to pay the post charges to Bath! And if I ask Papa to give me such a sum at this hour of the night, he will certainly demand to know what I want it for!"

It was at that moment that the thought of Lord Wilfrid came into her head.

Lord Wilfrid, said a cool, triumphantly logical voice inside that head, wished to take her to Bristol. Lord Wilfrid had a phaeton and fast horses. Bristol was some dozen miles from Bath. Once in Bristol, she could no doubt manage to persuade his lordship on some pretext or other to take her to Bath. Once in Bath she could rescue Campaspe and send Lord Wilfrid to the right-about.

It all worked out as neatly as a problem in

mathematics, and if Lord Wilfrid somewhat unfairly came off with all kicks and no ha'pence, as her old nurse had used to say, that, she considered, was his own fault for having paid no attention to what the gypsy had told him at the races that afternoon.

"Aye, *serve the purpose*—that's the word for *you*, fair gentleman," the gypsy had said, and had offered to save him a deal of trouble by reading his palm—a reading which no doubt would have revealed to him the fact that he was about to be made use of by an unscrupulous young woman.

"But—very well! If I must be unscrupulous to save Campaspe, I shall be unscrupulous!" thought Gwendolen defiantly; and, refolding the note and replacing it in her reticule, she went off to the ballroom to find Lord Wilfrid.

This was not difficult to do, for Lord Wilfrid, having apparently decided not to take offence at her abrupt departure, but to put her lack of politeness in taking leave of him down to the natural perturbation of a female upon finding something amiss with her dress in a public place, was standing just where she had left him, awaiting her return.

"Oh, Lord Wilfrid!" she addressed him at once, speaking in the best counterfeit she could call up at the moment of a young lady in a state of considerable romantic confusion. "*Pray* forgive me for leaving you so suddenly, but I found, when it came to the point, that I required a few moments in which to compose myself! You see, I have made up my mind!" She looked up soulfully into Lord Wilfrid's face, which understandably bore a faintly puzzled frown upon it, and murmured, "Venice! With *you*! Only it must be at once, my—my dearest Wilfrid!

Tonight! This very moment! I feel my courage will desert me else!"

Lord Wilfrid had a well-earned reputation in the Polite World for an aplomb unshakable under any circumstances — a reputation once put to the severest of tests when a young woman who had formerly been under his protection had forced her way past the porter at White's and confronted him in the card room with an extremely vocal and highly profane demand for money before an assemblage that had included two Royal Dukes. But even Lord Wilfrid looked momentarily nonplussed upon being faced during the course of a ball with a call for an immediate elopement, made by a young lady who only that afternoon had spurned the very idea of one in no uncertain terms.

"My *dearest* Gwen —" he drawled, sparring for wind, as his fellow habitués at Gentleman Jackson's Bond Street Boxing Saloon might have expressed it. "My dear girl — *tonight*? You can't mean, literally —"

"Oh, but I do!" Gwendolen said fervently, "It is just what I *do* mean! *Do* take me away at once, dear Wilfrid, or I *know* I shall never screw up my courage to the sticking point again! You *said* the Duke's yacht was ready to sail —"

"And so it is," Lord Wilfrid acknowledged, "but — you have not come prepared? Your clothes — necessaries — ?"

"Oh, I care nothing for *that*," declared Gwendolen, brushing aside the very thought of these mundane matters. She seized upon a phrase from Campaspe's note. "Besides, I am sure *you* will provide for me!"

Lord Wilfrid, who had regained something of his poise by this time, said gallantly that he would be delighted to do so, but he nevertheless appeared about to raise some

further cavils to this impetuous elopement when Gwendolen, who had learned in the nursery that she had the
valuable asset, usually given only to those people who
seldom cry at all, of bringing tears to her eyes at will, did
so.

"Oh, *please!*" she said imploringly. "If I do not go now,
I shall never, never have the courage again, and you can't
know how tired I am of this horrid, humdrum existence!"

Lord Wilfrid looked down at the pleading blue eyes
under those enchanting, flyaway black brows, the crystal
drops just overflowing them and making them seem as
bright and soft as stars on a summer night. He opened his
mouth to speak and then closed it again. Obviously,
when one had the bird in one's net, one did not tempt
fortune by letting it go free on the foolish assumption
that one might catch it again when it might be more convenient to do so. And an immediate elopement, after all,
presented few problems with which he was not prepared
to cope.

"Very well, my dearest!" he said, making up his mind.
"Tonight it shall be, then! Should you object to driving to
Bristol in my phaeton? My travelling chaise is at
Beauworth—"

Gwendolen said hastily that she had not the least objection to the phaeton, and could they start at once?—to
which Lord Wilfrid agreed, stipulating only that they
must first stop at the George, where he was putting up, so
that he might provision himself for the journey.

Gwendolen then suddenly bethought herself of the fact
that she would be abandoning Jane at the ball with absolutely no clew as to what had happened to her two
sisters unless she left her a note. So she requested Lord
Wilfrid to send a servant for ink and paper, which he did

rather reluctantly, having found, in a wide experience in such matters, that it was far better to wait, as he had once expressed it, until the *fait* was *accompli* before letting any third party into the secret.

But Gwendolen was adamant, promising, however, not to confide any of the details of the elopement to Jane, which in point of fact she had no intention of doing. Indeed, Lord Wilfrid would have been a good deal surprised and even mystified had he been able to peruse the hastily scrawled missive that she entrusted to the servant who had brought her the writing materials, with instructions to wait at least a half hour before giving it into the hands of Miss Jane Quarters.

Dearest Jane, it ran, *Cammie has got herself into a scrape and I am off to rescue her. It is probable we shan't return until morning, but pray tell Mama and Papa that there is nothing for them to fly up into the boughs about. I shall take good care of Cammie. Gwen.*

It occurred to her, as she penned this missive, that she had no clear idea as to how she and Cammie were to return from Bath to Cheltenham with no more than a few shillings between them; but she did not allow this consideration to trouble her for long. After all, there was always Lord Wilfrid, and then Lyndale would be there as well. If she could not succeed, she thought, in at least procuring coach-fare from one of these two guilty would-be seducers, she must consider herself a downright widgeon!

Sixteen

Meanwhile, Campaspe was speeding most romantically in Lyndale's curricle under a thundery night sky towards Gloucester, where her bridegegroom-to-be (or at least so he figured in her mind) turned his horses' heads south along the Bristol pike road.

It might have occurred to a disinterested observer, however, that for a bridegroom-to-be, his lordship was displaying a most unloverlike lack of interest in his passenger. He rarely addressed her, occupying much of his time instead in whistling cheerfully as he guided his team expertly along the dark road. Campaspe, however, was not a disinterested observer, nor was she (as she was discovering somewhat to her own surprise as she was being borne swiftly along towards Bath and her future destiny as the Marchioness of Lyndale) the coolly calculating young woman, cynically determined upon making a highly advantageous match for the sake of her family, that she had imagined herself to be during the past several hours.

When Lyndale, as they had found themselves briefly alone at the races that afternoon while walking from his curricle to the Duke of Tardiff's marquee, had replied to one of her outrageously inviting sallies with a sudden and entirely matter-of-fact proposal that they elope to Bath that very evening, Campaspe had at first felt nothing but triumph. How easy it had been, she told herself in smug self-congratulation, to solve at one fell swoop all the problems that had been driving everyone in the family, from worldly wise Aunt Pris to poor woollyheaded Jane, almost to distraction over the past week.

She had gone home in a whirl of plots and mystery, and it was not until after she was actually at the Assembly Rooms and the musicians had struck up the music for the second set, during which she and Lyndale proposed to leave the ball and set out upon their journey to Bath, that cold fingers of doubt had first clutched her heart. A little later, mounting into Lyndale's curricle, it had suddenly come upon her with the blinding force of revelation that all she really wished to do was to run home to her mother, hide her face in that maternal bosom, and cry as heartily as Jane had ever cried over Alain de Combray.

It was not, she told herself vehemently, that, like Jane, she wished to marry someone else! No, indeed! Nothing of that sort entered into the matter! But somehow the idea of going through the rest of her life as a marchioness, which had seemed, on the whole, a rather alluring thought, had suddenly become far less attractive, now that it was upon the point of becoming a reality, and even the excitment of participating in a midnight elopement, exactly like the heroine in a novel, appeared to have lost its romantic charm. To tell the truth, she did not feel in the least romantic, but only a little frightened and slightly sick.

The cheerful profile of her uncommunicative lover, at which she stole a glance from time to time, did little to reassure her. The thoughts occurred to her, in fact, in disagreeable sequence, that after all she knew very little about the Marquis of Lyndale, that no doubt one picked up some very queer ideas about marriage in Morocco — or was it Algeria? — and that Bluebeard might very well have whistled quite as cheerfully as Lyndale was doing as he conducted his latest victim to his castle.

There were thirty-four miles of good pike road from Gloucester to Bristol — a circumstance that had no doubt induced the Marquis to choose that route instead of taking the shorter, but very bad road that led south by way of Nailsworth, and the curricle sped along at a spanking pace, his lordship's own peerless team of Welsh greys, as he had informed her, being good for two stages, so that they were obliged to change horses only once, at Falfield, before they reached Bristol.

Here, unfortunately, rain, which had been threatening all the way south from Gloucester, began to fall rather heavily as they turned east towards Bath. Campaspe's spirits suddenly rose. The arrangements for their marriage, it occurred to her, had been made for Bath, and if they should be prevented from reaching that town by the inclemency of the weather, it would certainly be impossible, at this hour of the night, for Lyndale to find a clergyman to perform the ceremony elsewhere.

And if, she asked herself, her spirits rising even further, the fatal knot were not actually tied that night, how could one know what obstacles might arise to prevent it from ever being tied at all? Her father, apprised by Gwendolen of the contents of the note she had left behind her, might come after them, breathing fire and pro-hibitions; even Neil, a small hopeful voice inside her said, might somehow learn what she was proposing to do and decide that, in spite of their horrid quarrel, he could not bear to have her marry someone else and arrive, like young Lochinvar, to snatch her from Lyndale's arms at the last moment.

"We shall have to stop now — shan't we?" she enquired of Lyndale, putting her hopes into words as the rain pelted down upon them more heavily and she huddled under the rug with which he had provided her.

"Stop? Why so?" Lyndale said encouragingly. "Who ever heard of stopping an elopement for a little rain?"

"But it isn't *a little* rain," Campaspe pointed out. "It is pouring." She added, in as coaxing a tone as she could manage, "I am getting very wet, and I really *should* like to stop, my lord."

"My lord? You are very formal!" said Lyndale, con-tinuing to drive on quite as rapidly as before. "Wouldn't you feel it more appropriate to say David at this stage of the game?"

Campaspe frowned. Neil, she felt sure, would not have replied to a perfectly reasonable request from her to be taken in out of a heavy rain by making inappropriate remarks about his name.

"David, then," she said rather shortly, and continued with some emphasis, "and I should really like to stop. There must be any number of inns in Bristol."

"I am quite sure that there are, but *we* are not going to stop at any of them," said the Marquis with infuriating calm. "You forget, my love, that there is a clergyman awaiting us at the White Hart in Bath, and that without his services we shall not be able to be married tonight."

Campaspe said rebelliously that they could be married just as well tomorrow, and that meanwhile they would at least not be taking their death of cold.

"Nonsense!" said his lordship bracingly. "A fine, healthy girl like you doesn't take her death of cold so easily."

"Well," said Campaspe vengefully, acknowledging defeat as Lyndale kept his horses moving as steadily as before towards Bath, "I can tell you one thing: you ought to be very glad you aren't eloping with Jane. *She* would have the vapours if you kept *her* out in this weather."

Lyndale said politely that in that case he was very glad, too, that Jane was not to be his bride, and then compounded the injury implicit in the offhand manner in which he had made this remark by observing that he thought she, Campaspe, would take to camel-riding in Morocco rather better than Jane would, as well.

"Are—are we going to Morocco?" Campaspe asked in a somewhat faltering voice. Four-and-twenty hours ago, she knew, she would have jumped with joy at the thought of exotic adventures in a foreign land, but somehow, sitting in the rain in the middle of the night beside a man who was, after all, a comparative stranger, and who was driving her inexorably towards married doom, the thought of leaving England, her sisters, her parents, and above all Neil, suddenly appeared fraught with danger to her. "I—I don't know that I should very much like that," she said in a rather small voice. "I thought you wished to stay in England."

"Well, we shall at least go to Morocco on our wedding

trip," Lyndale said decisively. "No doubt you will find living in a harem very entertaining, at least for a time."

"In a — a harem!" Campaspe stared at him, horrified. "But — you have not got a harem!" she exclaimed. "Gwen says you told her so — "

"That is quite correct," Lyndale said equally. "At the present time I have *not* got a harem. But now that I have got in the way of being married, I see that there is perhaps some point in the saying that one can't have too much of a good thing. There is nothing for you to be concerned about upon that score, though," he added kindly. "As my *first* wife, you would of course bear the title of Marchioness of Lyndale, and your children would take precedence in inheriting the title."

Campaspe said nothing; indeed, at the moment she was so overwhelmed by a variety of emotions that she could not speak. Foremost among them seemed to be shocked disapproval, not to say outrage, at a pair of parents and an aunt who had been so blind as to thrust this man — or, rather, this monster — upon their respective daughter and niece as a suitable husband. That they had not thrust him upon her, but upon Jane, made it even worse, for Jane would have been far less capable than was she to cope with the situation, once she found herself in his clutches. She, Campaspe — so she vowed to herself, sitting huddled in the rain while Bath, the White Hart, and an unknown clergyman duped, or bribed, by Lyndale into assisting him in his fell purpose, came inexorably closer — would have the will and resolution to extricate herself from those clutches, if she had to make a scandal in doing so that would set all Bath by the ears.

She glanced over at Lyndale, who seemed quite content with her silence and, indeed, had gone back to whistling again. Should she, she debated, jump down from the curricle when they reached the White Hart and demand protection from the first person she encountered there? Unfortunately, at this hour of the night she would undoubtedly encounter no one but ostlers, and she was more than a little dubious about the response these essentially slow-witted and, she feared, unchivalrous persons would give to a request by a highly bedraggled young lady in evening dress to be rescued from the gentleman with whom she had driven into the yard.

It might be better, she thought upon consideration, to wait until she and Lyndale had entered the inn, where the landlord might appear, or at least some servant to whom she might appeal. And then there was the clergyman, of course, who perhaps had not the least notion that his services had been engaged for the purpose of marrying an innocent young girl to a fiend in human form who intended to carry her off to Morocco and shut her up in a harem.

On the whole, however, she was more inclined to place her dependance upon the landlord or the servant, as the clergymen involved in such situations in the lending-library novels she had read had frequently turned out not to be clergymen at all, but tools of the villain in clerical disguise.

By the time she had come to these conclusions, the curricle had covered the dozen miles between Bristol and Bath, and they were entering the sleeping town. All too soon Stall Street and the White Hart were reached, and she found herself, with a beating heart, being assisted by Lyndale, who had flung the reins to a sleepy ostler, to alight from the curricle. He was smiling, she saw, as she mistrustfully gave him her hand, but it was a smile that struck a chill to her heart. Others, she thought, might merely see a handsome man with very blue eyes and a determined chin when they looked at him, but *she* knew the fiendish plans that lurked behind that agreeable smile and that prepossessing face.

"Come along," he urged her. "You will be warm and dry in a trice, and then we shall see about this wedding."

Campaspe, propelled towards the door by a strong hand under her elbow, said inspirationally, grasping at straws, that she was very hungry.

"Good! You shall have a splendid wedding breakfast after the ceremony," Lyndale assured her. "The very best the White Hart has to offer."

"But I—I feel *quite* famished now." Campaspe said, glancing desperately about her as she was impelled across the inn yard towards the entrance. But the ostler had already unharnessed the horses and disappeared in the direction of the stable, and the only living creature she saw was a very large black cat gazing crossly out at the rain as it crouched beneath the shelter of a farm cart. "I *really* think I ought to have something to eat at once," she went on to Lyndale, as her reluctant feet approached the door.

She was interrupted by the sound of a sudden clatter of hooves behind her. A lathered horse was galloping full tilt into the inn-yard, and as its rider reined it in and hastily jumped down, shouting for an ostler to take it in charge, Campaspe, with a thrill of joy, recognised a familiar voice and figure.

"Neil! Neil!" she cried, pulling her arm free of Lyndale's grasp and running across the inn-yard towards the new arrival. "Oh, Neil, you *have* come to save me! Oh, *do* take me away!"

And she flung herself so impetuously into young Lieutenant Fairhall's arms that, almost bowled over, he saved himself from falling only by embracing her as tightly as she was embracing him.

"Here — don't knock a fellow off his feet, flying at him like a dashed hurricane!" he remonstrated. "You're all right now. Where's Lyndale? I must speak to him at once!"

To Campaspe's indignation, he hastily detached her clinging arms from him and turned to the Marquis, who had also come across the inn-yard in long strides and was now regarding him grimly.

"What the devil does this mean, Fairhall?" he demanded, before Neil could open his mouth to speak. "Where is Miss Quarters?"

Campaspe looked from one to the other of them in astonishment.

"Miss Quarters?" she said. "Do you mean Gwen? What has she — ?"

But her questions were overborne by Neil, who, disregarding them completely, said quickly, in an agitated voice, to Lyndale, "I don't know where she is, sir! I came as fast as I could to tell you — cross-country, and the deuce of a ride it was by night! You see, she gave me the slip before I could carry out our plan, and by the best I can learn, she has gone off with Lord Wilfrid Boulting!"

"The *devil* you say!"

Campaspe, hearing the sudden harsh note in his lordship's voice and seeing the menacing glint in his blue eyes, thought, with a little shudder of relief at her escape, that he probably really *was* a Bluebeard; but relief was almost immediately driven out of her mind by the equally strong emotions of curiosity and anxiety that young Lieutenant Fairhall's peculiar remarks about Gwendolen had aroused in her.

"Gone off with Lord Wilfrid! But she *can't* have —" she began, at the same moment that Lyndale continued, in that same urgent voice, to Neil, "Gone off where? And why? Speak up, boy! You don't mean to tell me she has eloped with him?"

Neil, who was now looking extremely guilty as well as agitated, said he couldn't tell, but it looked very much to him as if that was the case.

"When I went to find her — exactly as we had arranged, sir! — she had simply disappeared, you see," he said. "So I began asking questions, and some people said they had seen her leaving with Lord Wilfrid, and then I went outside and asked the coachmen, and *they* said she's driven off with him in his phaeton and that he'd looked devilish pleased with himself, and why not, with such a prime article smiling up at him like he was the Regent himself — Well, you know how they *will* talk, sir, and I'm only repeating it because it seems to show how the land lies."

The Marquis swore, briefly but effectively. "*Damn* the girl!" he said. "I might have known she'd throw us all into a bumblebath somehow or other! And why the *devil*," he added sternly to Neil, "didn't you try at once to find the direction they had taken, instead of haring off here to Bath?"

"B-but I thought — Campaspe —" Neil stammered. "You said — You'd planned —"

"What I'd planned was to have you bring Miss Quarters here!" Lyndale said scathingly. "You knew Campaspe was safe enough with me! If you'd had the brains of a monkey, you'd have realised that it was Miss Quarters who stood in need of your protection!"

"But she *wanted* to elope with him," Neil protested, defending himself. "He couldn't force her to go with him! And a fine nodcock I should have looked, trying to interfere between them—"

"You look a fine nodcock now, my lad," Lyndale said grimly, "for you've made mice feet of this business and no mistake! Now listen to me! I'm off for Cheltenham at once, and as for you, you are going to strike off north as fast as you can! If he intends marriage, they may take the Great North Road to Gretna; but it's more likely, I think, that marriage is the last thing he has in mind, and in that case he may have taken her anywhere! I shall have to try to pick up a clew in Cheltenham." He drew out his pocketbook, extracted several bank-notes from it, and thrust them into Campaspe's hands. "Here—take this!" he said. "You will find a private parlour and bedchamber bespoke in my name inside; you may stop here for the night, and in the morning take a post-chaise back to Cheltenham."

Campaspe, who was by this time so totally bewildered by the events of the past few minutes that all she could really grasp was the fact that Lyndale had apparently not the least intention of marrying her that night, and instead was bent upon rescuing Gwendolen from Lord Wilfrid, blinked at the money in her hand.

"But I don't understand!" she said vehemently. "Why was Neil to bring Gwen here tonight? And why has she run off with Lord Wilfrid? And why—?"

"There's no time for that now," Lyndale said peremptorily. "Go on into the inn! Fairhall, fetch one of those ostlers and tell him I want a fresh team figged out—"

He broke off abruptly as a smart phaeton, spattered generously with mud, turned into the inn-yard at a gallop. It was driven by a gentleman in evening dress under a drab benjamin; a lady, likewise formally attired and wrapped in a rug, sat beside him.

"Gwen!" cried Campaspe, recognising her eldest sister, as the lady, scarcely waiting for the horses to be brought to a halt, jumped down from the phaeton.

Gwendolen, seeing her standing there transfixed in the light of the carriage lamps, came towards her quickly across the cobblestones.

"Cammie!" she exclaimed in tones of the greatest relief, sweeping her sister into a protective embrace. "Thank God I have come up with you before it is too late! Dearest, you have been duped! Lyndale has no intention of marrying you!" She caught sight of the Marquis, who also seemed to be transfixed by some strong emotion as he stood beside Campaspe, and surveyed him with a scorching glance. "Let me tell you, sir," she addressed him scathingly, "that I consider your conduct infamous, and that if I were a man, I should certainly take it upon myself to demand satisfaction of you! Attempting to seduce an innocent young girl—" She broke off suddenly as she became aware of the presence of Lieutenant Fairhall, also standing transfixed beside the others in the rain. "Neil!" she exclaimed in tones of the greatest disbelief. "What are *you* doing here? How did *you* know what Lyndale was planning to do? Did you come to rescue Cammie? And if you did, why haven't you—?"

"Very well—that's quite enough now!" Lyndale cut in, in tones of authority not unmixed with amusement. In point of fact, he seemed, to Gwendolen's resentful eyes, to have got over the disconcerting effect of her abrupt

194

arrival upon the scene with remarkable rapidity, and now appeared to find the situation one of high comedy rather than of high drama. "We had best discuss all of this inside," he said, "where we can dry ourselves before a comfortable fire, for I foresee that it may take considerable time to sort this tangle out. And, at any rate, the Reverend Mr. Broadfute may be growing a trifle impatient. So come along, Miss Quarters — Campaspe — Fairhall," he addressed them in turn. "You, too, Wilfrid," he added, turning with a sudden touch of grimness in his voice to Lord Wilfrid. "I should like very much to have *your* part in this affair explained to me."

Lord Wilfrid, who had given a sort of convulsive start at the mention of a clergyman — a point that appeared to absorb him to the extent that even the scarcely veiled menace in Lyndale's last words seemed to have no effect upon him — hastily said, no, he wouldn't go inside, as it was quite imperative for him to return to Bristol that night.

"I — I am going abroad, you see," he said, backing away in a rather crablike fashion towards his phaeton. "And as Miss Campaspe appears to be quite safe — "

To the astonishment of several of the parties present, who had never seen his aplomb so shattered, he then made a kind of dash for the phaeton, snatched the reins from the gaping ostler, and drove out of the inn-yard, whipping up his horses as if the devil himself were after him.

"What in the world is the matter with *him?*" asked Campaspe in awestruck tones.

"Oh, I daresay he did not like the sound of a clergyman," Gwendolen said tolerantly. "I let him think he was eloping with me in order to get him to take me to

195

Bristol, you see, and then when we had arrived there, I was obliged to speak to him very strongly so that he would agree to take me on here to rescue you, Cammie. I expect it made him rather nervous, and not quite capable of thinking things through properly, so that when he heard there was a clergyman involved, he was afraid I might have made him marry me." She looked at Lyndale accusingly. "Of course, it is a *sham* clergyman, and he is your accomplice in this dastardly plot of yours to seduce my sister," she said.

Lyndale's shoulders were shaking, though he was making a valiant attempt to control his mirth. "Oh, Gwen, Gwen, my darling Gwen, how could I ever have imagined that you wouldn't be more than a match for Wilfrid?" he said. "He'll never get over this—"

"What do you mean—'my darling Gwen'?" Gwendolen interrupted him wrathfully. "I am *not* your darling, my lord!"

"Oh yes, you are!" declared Lyndale. "Whether you wish to be or not! You have been so since the first moment I set eyes on you. But come inside out of this rain and I'll explain it all to you. I have made a devilish muddle of it, it seems, but after all you can't hang a man for trying!"

Seventeen

The landlord of the White Hart, who had been roused out of peaceful slumber by the sound of an unusual amount of activity in his inn-yard in the middle of a stormy and disagreeable night, was even further astonished to see walk into his inn shortly afterwards four persons in evening dress: two ladies and two gentlemen, all obviously Quality and all extremely wet.

The taller of the gentlemn, introducing himself as the Marquis of Lyndale, at once demanded that they be shown to the private parlour that had been bespoken in his name, and, when this had been accomplished, issued orders concerning the building up of the fire and the bringing of suitable spirituous liquors with which to ward off the possibility of any of the company's taking a chill, that sent the landlord scurrying for his minions.

When these orders had been fulfilled, Gwendolen, who

had ignored Lyndale's invitation to seat herself in one of the comfortable Windsor armchairs but had stationed herself instead before the fireplace with something of the air of a judge waiting for the criminal to be brought before him, said in an extremely chilly tone to Lyndale that if he had any explanation of his conduct, he had best give it now.

"Yes, I daresay I had," Lyndale agreed amicably. "The only thing is, I don't know quite where to begin, and, also, I refuse to say a word until you have taken some of this brandy. It's not necessary for you to stay stone-cold sober in order to ring a peal over me, you know," he added, as Gwendolen appeared to be about to give voice to a determination to have nothing to do with any brandy provided by so black a scoundrel. "In fact, I shouldn't wonder if you made an ever better job of it if you had some of this first."

As he spoke, he had poured a generous amount of brandy into a glass, which he now offered to her, and Gwendolen, deciding that for Campaspe's sake she must not take a chill that would deprive her of her protection, accepted it with an air of hauteur and took a cautious sip.

"I have no desire to *ring a peal over you*, as you express it, Lord Lyndale," she said, with as grand a manner as Lady Otilia herself could have managed. "Your conscience, I should think, would tell you how badly you have behaved. To plan to seduce an innocent young girl — "

"Now look here," said the Marquis, interrupting her without heat but with considerable emphasis, "that's the second time you've said that, and it won't do, you know. I haven't been planning to seduce anyone, innocent or

198

otherwise. In fact, all I have really been trying to do is to marry you."

"To marry *me!*" If a bomb had exploded in the cosy parlour at that moment, blowing the well-polished table and chairs to bits and sending the ceiling crashing down upon her head, Gwendolen could not have felt more surprise. The surprise in that case, however, would scarcely have had the effect of sending the kind of delicious thrill down her backbone that the Marquis's words had produced, an effect somewhat similar to the first stages of intoxication, which she at once put down to the brandy. "I do not think, Lord Lyndale," she said, hastily collecting herself and succeeding in speaking almost as icily as before, "that this is a suitable moment for jesting!"

"But I'm *not* jesting!" Lyndale assured her, with a rather rueful grin. "Oh, I'll admit I've made a proper mull of it, but my intentions were beyond reproach. Here—look at these!" he adjured her, drawing from his pocket a pair of folded documents, which he proceeded to lay before her upon the table. "Do you know what these are?"

"No, nor do I care to," said Gwendolen superbly.

But Campaspe, in whom curiosity was far stronger than resentment, picked them up and, after examining them critically, said she thought they were special licences.

"But why two?" she demanded. "You needn't have one each for the bride and the bridegroom, need you? I thought one was enough to marry two people."

Lyndale said she was quite correct on that point, but that as he had hoped that *two* weddings might be performed that night, he had therefore been obliged to procure two licences. Campaspe, who had been looking much more cheerful ever since Lieutenant Fairhall's arrival upon the scene, at this point relapsed into horrified apprehension once more.

"*Oh!*" she exclaimed. "Do you mean you were planning to marry both me *and* Gwen? But you *couldn't*—not here in England! You *can't* set up a harem in England!"

"Don't be a goose, Cammie!" said Gwendolen severely. "Of course Lord Lyndale had no intention of marrying either you *or* me. No doubt these documents are forged."

"You *will* think the worst of me, won't you?" complained his lordship. "And after I spent a devilish dreary week and more in London making all these arrangements! Do you know you can't get a special licence from anyone but a bishop? And as for young Alain de Combray—he may be a very personable, intelligent halfling, with some of the bluest blood in France in his veins, but finding someone who is willing to help him to a place suitable to his talents is one of the labours of Hercules to a man who has been out of Europe as long as I have! Fortunately, I am well acquainted with General Lord Cathcart, and through his interest I have been able to assure young M. de Combray of a position that will allow him to take a wife and presently, I hope, to progress up the ladder in the diplomatic service. It will mean, of course, that you will be obliged to part with your sister Jane for a time, since his first assignment will take him to Brazil, but I am sure that for the sake of her happiness you will undergo the separation cheerfully—" He broke off, observing that Gwendolen was looking at him with an absolutely dumbfounded expression upon her face. "Is something the matter?" he enquired politely.

"The matter!" Gwendolen strove for words. "Of course there is something the matter!" she said. "Do you mean to stand there and tell us, my lord, that you—*you!*—have interested yourself in finding a position for Alain de Combray so that he will be able to marry Jane?"

"Well, it seemed the only way to make sure you wouldn't expect me to marry her myself, you see," Lyndale explained. "I know Campaspe has always been very much set against that, but I had an idea that you, on the other hand, might have held it against me if Jane had found herself without a husband while I went off and married someone else. In point of fact," he added, "that was my reason for arranging to have Campaspe married tonight, as well. Knowing your peculiar sense of family loyalty, my darling Gwen, I thought you might expect me to respond to her determined courtship by marrying her, too—I mean, of course," he added hastily, seeing from the expression upon Campaspe's face that it was possible she would regard this statement as an invitation to begin talking about harems again—" *instead* of Jane. At any rate, I thought I should feel safer if she were married, too."

"Married to *who?*" Campaspe asked, her brow very much furrowed as she attempted to follow the drift of his lordship's conversation. "You *can't* mean—to Neil!"

"Can't I?"

A slow, furious flush arose in Campaspe's cheeks. "Do you mean—*do you mean* that you never had any intention of marrying me yourself?" she enquired wrathfully. "That you brought me here tonight to marry me to *Neil?*"

"Well, it didn't turn out exactly as I had planned it, you see," Lyndale said apologetically. "Fairhall was to arrive in the nick of time to rescue you from me, after which you would of course fall into his arms and, a clergyman and a special licence being providentially at hand, agree to reward him by bestowing yourself upon him in matrimony. But I'm afraid that both Fairhall and I were so disconcerted by your sister's apparent elopement with Wilfrid that we neglected to act our parts properly — "

He broke off, for Campaspe had turned upon the tall young lieutenant with very much the air of an infuriated kitten about to launch itself into an attack upon a large, innocent dog.

"Neil Fairhall!" she addressed him in militant tones. "You are a *traitor*! To — to conspire against me with this — this — "

"But it isn't conspiring against you to want to marry you, Cammie," the young lieutenant protested feebly. "And, dash it all, how else was I to bring it off? You've turned a cold shoulder to me ever since we had that silly disagreement — "

"It *wasn't* a silly disagreement! You said I was making a cake of myself and that you didn't want to be married to me!" Campaspe said vengefully. "And if you think for a single moment that you and Lyndale between you are clever enough to trick me into marrying you — well, you had best think twice, is all I can tell you!" She trod over to Gwendolen, who was still standing before the fireplace. "Come, Gwen!" she said superbly. "Let us go! No doubt Lieutenant Fairhall and Lord Lyndale will be able to think of some stratagem between them by which they can persuade two females more credulous than we are to marry them, so they will not be obliged to waste those very expensive licences!"

There was nothing, Gwendolen told herself, that she would have liked better than to order up a post-chaise and a pair of horses and, shaking the dust of the White Hart from her shoes, return to Cheltenham with her sister. Unfortunately the same circumstance that had required her to make use of Lord Wilfrid in pursuing Campaspe prevented her from doing so: she had not sufficient funds. She gazed in frustration from Lyndale to Lieutenant Fairhall, and then, choosing the latter as the lesser of two evils, said to him in dignified tones, "I fear I must request a loan of you, sir. If you will allow me to have a sufficient sum to hire a post-chaise to take my sister and myself back to Cheltenham—"

"No, you don't, my lad!" said Lyndale promptly, as Neil began obediently to pull out his pocketbook. "If we let them get away now, we'll be bachelors for the rest of our lives." He turned to Gwendolen. "I am extremely sorry, Miss Quarters," he said to her with great formality, "but at one and tuppence per mile for each horse, the sum required is quite beyond Lieutenant Fairhall's means."

"Coach-fare, then!" Gwendolen said, ignoring him and again addressing Lieutenant Fairhall. "You can't be so mean as to refuse us that!"

"Oh yes, he can!" Lyndale intervened once more. "Not a shilling, not a penny, not a farthing do you wheedle out of either of us, my girl! You have got yourselves into this, and the only way you will get out of it is by marrying us."

"Oh, I say!" protested Lieutenant Fairhall, unable to subscribe to this high-handed method of obtaining a bride; and at the same moment a deep, rumbling voice said apologetically behind them, "I fear my lord, that I come somewhat tardily upon my time. The truth is, I believe that, owing to the lateness of the hour, I fell into a light slumber—"

The entire company turned in surprise towards the door, where a rotund elderly gentleman in an old-fashioned, rusty, full-skirted coat, knee breeches, and square-toed, steel-buckled shoes, the whole with the rather rumpled appearance of having been slept in, stood blinking at them amiably. Lyndale, recovering himself first, moved towards him and shook him cordially by the hand.

"Ah, Mr. Broadfute!" he said. "Better late than never, as the saying goes! May I present Mr. Broadfute—Miss Quarters—Miss Campaspe Quarters—Lieutenant Fair-hall—"

Mr. Broadfute, beaming impartially upon the company, advanced upon Gwendolen and clasped her hand warmly in his, seeming quite oblivious of the very damp and somewhat dishevelled appearance she presented, with her fair hair curling in wild tendrils about her face and her rain-wet gown steaming gently before the fire. He then enquired, with an air of uttering a mild pleasantry, to which of the gentlemen before him he was to have the honour of uniting her in the bonds of holy matrimony— "for it does not do to err in these matters! No, indeed!" he concluded, with a jocosely meaningful look, which, however, elicited no suitable response from Gwendolen.

Instead, she withdrew her hand from his abruptly, and said, with a vehemence that surprised him a good deal, "To neither of them, sir! I have no wish to be married, nor has my sister!" She then astonished him even further by continuing, in the same earnest tone, "If you are indeed a clergyman, sir, I must appeal to you to assist us! My sister and I have been lured to this place by the grossest deception, and our only wish now is to return to our home in Cheltenham. Unfortunately, we have not sufficient money by us to pay post-chaises, or even coach-fare, and if you do not come to our aid, we shall be obliged to remain here, at the mercy of these — these — "

"Fiends?" Lyndale finished it for her politely. "Unfair, my Gwen! To the best of my knowledge, fiends do not offer lawful matrimony to their victims." He turned to Mr. Broadfute, whose round face now wore a troubled, not to say almost dumbfounded, look. "Pay no attention to Miss Quarters, sir," he said cheerfully. "She has not quite grown accustomed yet to the notion of being married tonight, you see, but I am sure she will come round if you will leave us alone for a few minutes — "

"No, I shan't!" said Gwendolen, outraged. "How *dare* you say such a thing, Lord Lyndale! I shouldn't marry you if — if — "

"*Not* if I were the last man alive, love!" Lyndale said reproachfully. "You know you wouldn't care to go through life a spinster. Besides, even if there were several other men alive — like Wilfrid, and the gallant Captain Belville — I still think you would do better to marry me. I'm reasonably good-tempered and intelligent; I *don't* keep a harem; nor have I any intentions along that line, in spite of what your sister will try to tell you; and I'm *not* a dead bore — at least, I don't think I am — "

To Gwendolen's horror and amazement, she found that it was on the tip of her tongue to say, "But you don't love me!" — and then burst at once into tears. Why she should be thinking of behaving in such an entirely foolish and outrageous manner she could not imagine, except that the shock of learning, after those wretched hours of suspense during which she had believed the Marquis to be set upon ruining her young sister, that his intention was to marry her, Gwendolen, instead had unhinged her reason.

But to her great relief she found that she still had sufficient control over herself to say in a very cool voice to Mr. Broadfute that she and her sister really did wish to return to Cheltenham as soon as possible, and that if he could see his way clear to lending them coach-fare, their father would reimburse him at the earliest feasible moment.

It was obvious, Gwendolen saw, as Mr. Broadfute's doubtful gaze met her own, than an impasse had now been reached. Apparently that reverend gentleman, in spite of his innocent and indeed rather woolly-headed air, had sufficient knowledge of the world to be aware that young ladies who have embarked upon runaway marriages frequently develop nerves and quite unreasonable fears, with the result that they behave in a manner that they are afterwards apt to regret. On the other hand, it was also obvious that he realised Gwendolen exhibited none of the signs of a female about to succumb to an attack of the vapours, and even more so was this true of Campaspe, for that young lady wore an extremely belligerent look and appeared capable of holding him up with a pistol, provided she could lay her hands upon one, and demanding his money if he did not give it to her.

Gwendolen saw, however, that Mr. Broadfute was also understandably a good deal in awe of his noble patron, and that it would go sorely against the grain with him to disoblige him in any way. But from this dilemma he was almost immediately rescued — or at least reprieved — by the sound of a commotion of some sort below stairs, following hard upon the rattle of carriage wheels in the inn-yard, which had gone all but unnoticed by the participants of the drama being enacted in the parlour above. A stentorian masculine voice was now heard to demand Lord Lyndale—a voice which seemed to rouse the liveliest amazement in the breasts of both the Misses Quarters.

"Papa!" they exclaimed simultaneously, while Lyndale, starting towards the door, said, "Quarters! And about time!"—and shouted to the landlord to show him up.

Eighteen

To the further astonishment of Gwendolen and Campaspe—but not, it seemed, of Lyndale—not only Mr. Quarters but Lady Otilia as well almost immediately appeared upon the threshold.

"Well, well!" said Mr. Quarters, surveying the scene before him with some satisfaction. "So we're all here eh? Is this your parson, Lyndale? Best get it over with, then. No need to keep us all up any longer. Devilish wet night. Time we were all in our beds."

Gwendolen and Campaspe merely stood staring at him. This, the former felt, was too much: after all the other shocks to which she had been subjected that night, to have her father and mother appear, like a *deus* and *dea ex machina* in a play, obviously prepared to assist at a double wedding ceremony, was more than flesh and blood could be expected to bear. She cast a look of burning reproach upon her parents, turned to Lyndale, and said, "You—you—!" in tones of extreme loathing, found she could think of no words in which to characterise properly his lordship's despicable behaviour, and walked out the nearest door.

It led into an adjoining bedchamber, which was fortunate, for one does not wish to cry in public. She was standing with her face buried in the red curtains when there was a step behind her, a pair of strong arms turned her gently about, and she found herself weeping against a coat of Bath superfine instead of against the curtains.

"I'm, sorry—sorry—sorry!" Lyndale's voice said above her. "I *have* made a mull of it—haven't I? I've gone too fast—taken far too much for granted—"

"You needn't think," Gwendolen said, mastering her sobs with difficulty and speaking with what dignity she could muster while she attempted ineffectually to release herself from those encircling arms, "that it is *you* who have made me cry, my lord. I am only crying because I am angry—and disappointed that Papa and Mama should have *conspired* with you against me—"

"Well, I'm afraid I rather dragooned them into it, you know," his lordship said apologetically, but making no move whatever to release her. "In the first place, I've offered them Brightleaves *and* your father's horses, and in the second place, they've had such a deuce of a time of it lately, what with all those broken engagements, that you can scarcely blame them for jumping at the chance to see two of their daughters married in one fell swoop. I made out a very good case for myself with them, I must say," he went on, with a sudden note of anxiety in his voice that for some reason made the tears well up in Gwendolen's eyes all over again. "Much better than I've done with you. I told them straight off that I'd been in love with you ever since I almost ran you down in the cursed lane and you came climbing up that bank looking at me like glorious murder—only, of course, I'd come to Gloucestershire to ask *Jane* to marry me, and what a devil's hank *that* put me in! I *couldn't* in honour draw back when I'd gone so far—but let me tell you, I was never so happy in my life as when I saw that *she* wanted the match no more than I. If I could have offered her young Frenchman half my fortune to take her off my hands, I'd have done it—but one can't manage matters quite so high-handedly as that—"

"No!" said Gwendolen, suddenly regaining her spirit and determinedly freeing herself from Lyndale's embrace. "Of course one can't do *that*! But it was quite all right, I daresay, for you to lure my young sister here with a promise of marriage that you had no intention of keeping, and to plot with Neil to bring *me* here so you could oblige me to marry you—"

"I thought you would want to," said his lordship simply, which piece of brazen effrontery so incensed Gwendolen that she was quite without words for a moment.

"Do you mean to imply, my lord," she said icily, when she had got her breath back, "that I encouraged you in any way? I deny it!"

"Well, you didn't cast out lures to me, if that's what you mean," Lyndale acknowledged. "You were the soul of propriety. But your eyes weren't, you know."

"My eyes!"

"Yes. One can't very well help what one's eyes say, and yours were always talking to me; in fact, they told me the first time I met you that you were almost as interested in me as I was in you." Gwendolen opened her mouth to utter an outraged denial, but Lyndale stopped her with an upflung hand. "Come—be honest with me!" he said. "Am I speaking the truth or not?"

His eyes met hers. She felt her defences crumbling and turned hastily away.

"*Why* I should be honest with such a black-souled liar as you I don't know!" she said with asperity. "But—yes, it's true! Only of course I couldn't let you—or even myself—know because of Jane—"

"Jane—Jane—Jane!" said the Marquis. "I wish I'd never laid eyes on the girl! Even better, I wish you'd never had a sister of any kind, for they've got devilishly in the way of my courtship, I can tell you! If it hadn't been for them, and for my feeling I should have to settle *them* before I settled with you, I shouldn't have been obliged to embark on this absurd plot in the first place."

Gwendolen, who had for some reason felt that it behooved her to place as great a distance as possible between herself and the Marquis, once she had made her dangerous admission concerning her feelings, found at this moment that Lyndale definitely had other ideas on the matter, for while he had been speaking, he had followed her across the room and now contrived to gather her—quite against her will, of course—once more into his arms.

"No—you mustn't!" she gasped, a good deal shaken but still manning her defences after his lordship had taken most unfair advantage of their close proximity to kiss her. "I *won't* be married in such a—such a *hugger-mugger* way! In the middle of the night, in an inn—"

"But with your papa and mama very properly in attendance—don't forget that!" Lyndale reminded her. "Not even the busiest gabblemonger can find matter for

211

scandel-broth in *that*." He held her off at arm's length for a moment and regarded her severely. "After all the trouble I've taken to marry you in the proper style, I *do* think you might be more grateful!" he said. "Besides apologising to me for all the aspersions you've cast upon my character—"

"I don't think you have any character! To make up such an abominable plot—you might have known it would come all to pieces! If you really are in l-love with me," Gwendolen went on, looking very attentively at the third button of his lordship's coat instead of into his face as she spoke, "why couldn't you have c-courted me properly—?"

"And run the risk, meanwhile, of Campaspe's behaving so outrageously that you and your entire family would say I had compromised her and ought to marry *her? Or* see you float off into an entanglement with another naval gentleman who happened to put you in mind of Lord Nelson? No, thank you!" said Lyndale emphatically. "You know what Shakespeare says— 'If it were done when 'tis done, then 'twere well it were done quickly,' or words to that effect—"

He broke off, as a confused babble of sound that had been steadily rising behind the door to the parlour reached a kind of climax and then halted abruptly as the door opened and Lady Otilia came into the room.

"Really, my lord," she said, regarding with some disapproval the tableau before her, showing her her eldest daughter clasped firmly in the marquis's embrace, "this is most improper, you know, to say nothing of the fact that you are keeping us all waiting! Here I have been having the most dreadful time of it, with Campaspe absolutely refusing to marry Neil Fairhall and Mr. Quarters roaring at her—for which I can scarcely blame him, for it *is* almost dawn and we had a *most* disagreeable journey in the rain—only fortunately Neil stood up to him and said Campaspe needn't marry him if she didn't wish to, so then, of course, she said she would, which is *just* like Campaspe. And now that *that* is settled, here you are dawdling and keeping poor Mr. Broadfute waiting—"

"Not dawdling," Lyndale said firmly. "Of that, Lady Otilia, you cannot accuse me. I have used every moment since I walked into this room in attempting to persuade your daughter to marry me—"

Gwendolen, by now grasping at straws and again ineffectually attempting to disengage herself from his lordship's arms, was heard to say something in a muffled voice to the effect that they had all thought it was Miss Courtney he wished to marry.

"Miss Courtney! Nonsense!" said Lady Otilia roundly. "*She* is engaged to marry the Duke. I heard of it only this evening—or last evening, I expect I should say by this time—while you were at the ball."

At any other time Gwendolen would have been so much interested in the news that Miss Courtney, obviously despairing at last of Lyndale, had astoundingly managed to induce the aging Duke of Tardiff to make her his Duchess that everything else would have flown straight out of her head; but now her only reaction to it was a feeling of slight annoyance with her mama for seeing fit to introduce a matter of such small importance into the conversation. It seemed to her that there was only one thing in the world that really mattered at that particular moment, and that was whether Lyndale would look at her again with the expression in his very blue eyes that had been there just before he had kissed her. Of course he wold not look at her like that while her mother was in the room, so it appeared that there was only one thing to be done.

"Mama," she said firmly to Lady Otilia, "go away."

"Go away!" Lady Otilia stared at her as if she had suddenly lost her senses. "Why should I go away?" she demanded. "You are not married yet, you know, Gwendolen! It would be most improper!"

"No, I am not married yet," Gwendolen agreed, but yielding not an inch. "And what is more to the point, I have not been proposed to, either."

Lady Otilia looked at her, at first with disapproval; but gradually a sibylline expression appeared upon her face.

"I see," she said simply, and turned her gaze upon Lyndale. "I trust, my lord, that you will be expeditious," she said to him. On the one hand, we women, of course, cherish these romantic occasions, but on the other hand, it is growing *very* late."

She then made a stately exit from the room. Lyndale, regarding his love with a quizzical expression upon his face, lost no time in leading her to a chair and going down upon one knee before her.

"Miss Quarters — Gwendolen," he pronounced punctiliously," may I humbly request you to do me the honour of bestowing upon me your hand and heart in marriage?"

Gwendolen frowned. "Well? Haven't I done it properly?" his lordship demanded. "I must say, you don't look very pleased."

"Quite properly," said Gwendolen, but still looking dissatisfied. "I daresay, like Mama, I am over-romantic—"

214

"You would prefer, I expect," said Lyndale agreeably, as he rose from his kneeling position, "that I do it like this"—and before she knew where she was he had raised her to her feet and swept her into an embrace that threatened imminent peril to her ribs. "Don't you know," said his lordship's voice presently, sounding quite different now both to her and to himself, probably because he had never kissed anyone before in a way that had had such an extremely satisfactory but definitely upsetting effect upon him, "that I *love* you—I *want* you—I *can't* do without you? If you would like me to put on a turban and a white robe and bear you off into the night on one of my Arabian steeds to satisfy your romantic inclinations, I am your man; but as it is still raining devilish hard outside and the mares are in Leicestershire, *would* you settle instead for a simple English ceremony presided over by Mr. Broadfute?"

Being Lady Otilia's daughter, there is little doubt that Gwendolen found his lordship's first offer an alluring one, but being also—as had been borne in upon her strongly during that disturbing kiss—very much in love, she was quite willing, even eager, to accept the second, with the result that in a very few minutes she was standing beside the Marquis in the parlour while Mr. Broadfute, now quite half asleep but with a beaming smile upon his face, prepared to read the marriage service over them.

"Gwen is the elder, so I daresay it is only proper she should be married first," said Campaspe in a loud whisper to her own betrothed, whose hand she was holding very tightly in case he might somehow get away again and she would be obliged to go and live in a harem.

"She *seems* quite resigned to having Lyndale, but after all he *has* been living in Morocco. Do you think one will be enough for him?"

"One what?" asked young Lieutenant Fairhall, who was not thinking very clearly himself at the moment, being highly involved with a dazed feeling of happiness combined with a terrified sensation that all this was not really happening to him and he would probably wake up at any moment.

"One wife, of course!" said Campaspe impatiently.

Lieutenant Fairhall, lending his mind to the question thus propounded, cast a sapient glance at the Marquis of Lyndale's face as he looked down at his bride, and after no more than a moment's consideration gave it as his emphatic opinion that *one* would definitely be quite enough.